I0552425

A CINDERELLA RETELLING

DEFIANT

A TALE OF CINDER
BOOK 1

M.J. HAAG

ISBN 978-1-943051-76-2 (eBook Edition)
ISBN 978-1-943051-20-5 (Paperback Edition)

The characters and events in this book are fictitious. Any similar to real persons, living or dead, is coincidental and not intended by the author.

Editing by Ulva Eldridge
Cover design by Shattered Glass Publishing LLC

FOREWORD

My love of fairy tales primarily revolved around Beauty and the Beast, and I'd never considered writing more retellings until my sister-from-another-mister (aka my sister-in-law), Dana, mentioned her love of Cinderella. If not for her, the world would have ended (well, the Beastly world anyway).

While Dana may have been the catalyst that caused the fairy tale continuation, there are others who help influence it. From the bottom of my heart, I thank Meg, Karen, Catherine, and Heather for their invaluable critique reads. Their feedback helped shape the story. Ulva, the super-amazing editor, who's been with me since almost the beginning, deserves a round of applause for smoothing out my rough writing edges, and my proof posse (Dawn, Jackie, Mirjam...you're the best team ever!) for catching all the little things I never see.

Finally, I thank my ARC team and all the fairy tale readers who can't resist another retelling. Without all of you, I wouldn't be writing.

INTRODUCTION

The Tales of Cinder are based on the original Brother's Grimm fairy tale, *The Little Glass Slipper*, with hints of *The Ash Tree Girl* by Marie de France. These old tales were often very dark and filled with some kind of "you better be good, or else" kind of morals. So, of course, I kept the Tales of Cinder dark, reimagining Cinder's journey of suffering and determination to reach her eventual happily ever. Hope you enjoy!

Magic can have deadly consequences.

When the sudden and suspicious death of Eloise's mother points to forbidden magic, Eloise is determined to bring her mother's murderer to justice. She will stop at nothing to find the killer...even if the clues lead right to the palace gates and the prince's manservant, Kaven. He is irrational, volatile, and prone to knocking women off horses. Given his personality, it should be easy to find the proof she needs to place him in irons.

However, when dark magic is used, nothing is as simple as it seems, and Eloise is about to learn that nightmares often hide behind fairy tale lives.

CHAPTER ONE

THE SUDDEN BAYING OF HOUNDS STARTLED THE CHICKENS AT my feet.

"Hugh?" I called, shaking the grain dust from my apron.

"Here, Miss Eloise." Our groomsman appeared from the stable, leading Sugar by her reins.

"Does that sound like hunting dogs?"

"It does." He nimbly leapt onto Sugar's back. "I'll go warn the hunters away."

As Hugh rode down the rutted path leading away from our small estate, I turned toward the two-storied house I called home. Smoke curled from all four chimneys, but with the hint of spring in the crisp air, I knew the fires wouldn't be necessary for long.

Letting myself into the kitchen, I inhaled the warm yeasty smell of the bread dough Judith was kneading.

"Were those hounds we heard?" she asked.

"Yes. Hugh went to warn the owners off." I shrugged out of my cloak and hung it and my apron by the door.

"It's been happening too frequently in recent years. The king should remind people that he cares about these lands by visiting them more often." Judith, who'd been with our family since I'd been born sixteen years ago, knew just how infrequently the king left his castle.

"I'm sure he has bigger concerns with Prince Granger's negotiations in the north," I said.

"What could we possibly need from the north?" Anne asked as she set a tray with a tea service for three.

"My guess is wool," Judith said. "In those colder temperatures, the herds probably have thicker coats."

While they spoke, I inspected the tray for something to eat.

"I was about to take this to the sitting room," Anne said, noting my interest. "Mrs. Cartwright requested you join her and your sister in there."

"You know Mother would be upset if she heard you calling her that," I said. "You're supposed to use her given name, Margaret."

"In her presence," Anne said with a small smile. "Elsewhere, I'll respectfully use her title."

I followed Anne from the kitchen, glad that Mother had selected her out of the many who had applied for the position. Already a widow, Anne was only two years older than me and didn't want anything other than security in life. Something Mother wanted for Kellen and myself. Something I had no interest in if it came in the form of a husband.

From the study, I heard the soft murmur of Kellen's voice as she read to Mother. She paused when Anne and I entered the room.

Mother reclined on a settee by the window. Although the sunlight gave her pale skin a healthier glow, the blankets that covered her body and pillows that propped her head bespoke the true state of her well-being. Yet, as much as Mother lived the life of an invalid, her gaze still alertly found mine.

"Hounds again?" she asked.

"So it seems," I answered, taking the seat near her.

Kellen shut her book and looked at me. My twin was my opposite in almost every way. Her straight ebony hair contrasted with my wavy golden tresses. The startling blue of her eyes, as well as her pale skin, held no warmth, whereas my golden tones were reflected in the warm hazel of my gaze. While I was quick to let the world know every emotion I felt, she held everything inside. I also towered over her petite frame by four inches, which I never used to my advantage. I never had to because Kellen and I didn't fight. Ever. Our differences did not make me love my sister less. No, I loved her more for each one.

I leaned forward and placed a kiss on my mother's soft cheek, surprising her.

"What's that for?"

"For giving me a sister instead of a brother. She would have been beastly as a boy."

"I would have been too small to be beastly," Kellen said evenly. "And tormented for my manly inadequacies. The only safe thing Mother could do for me was make me a girl."

Mother snorted, a smile ghosting her lips, our banter amusing her as I'd hoped it would.

"Speaking of manly attributes...did either of you notice any of interest when you went to market?" she asked. "I'd rather hoped there would be callers soon."

I gave Kellen a side glance. She kept her gaze focused on Mother.

"What?" Mother asked, catching the look. "What happened?"

"Nothing of importance, Mother," Kellen said. She looked at Anne, who'd been preparing our tea, and accepted the first cup for Mother. The milky brown liquid was laced with medicine.

"I won't drink that until you girls tell me what happened," Mother said. The surly note in her words made me smile.

"Well, we know it's not Father who gave me my temper," I said.

"You're right," Mother said, relaxing visibly. "It is better to nurture kindness in every thought and deed than to let even a cinder of anger smolder in your soul. For it only takes a cinder to start a fire." Then, she looked at me, love reflecting in her gaze.

"A fire can easily destroy what it took a lifetime to build."

"Or the face of a shopkeeper's son," Kellen added.

Mother made a pained expression.

"Oh, Eloise, what did you do?"

"I tested the sturdiness of the blacksmith's newest frying pan. I'm happy to report the smith was quite pleased with the results."

"You hit a boy with a frying pan?"

"Well, if you must put it so brashly...yes."

Anne made a small noise and quickly excused herself.

Mother stared at me for a moment before taking her tea from Kellen and drinking it down in several long swallows. She handed back the cup and closed her eyes.

"I'm ready for the full adventurous tale, my darlings."

Kellen and I shared a smile and launched into a recounting of our market visit from the day before. We embellished a few places for entertainment purposes, but never so much as to veer from the truth. The truth being that, years ago, Kellen and I had gradually gained a reputation of sorts with the boys in town. My quick to ignite temper had earned me the nickname of Cinder while Kellen's abidingly cool exterior had earned her the name Snow.

"When Carver lobbed a ball of muddy snow at Kellen, I grabbed the pan to block it; but my aim was off. While the ball splattered us, the pan hit Carver with a resounding gong that gained the attention of just about everyone on the street."

Mother snorted a laugh and held out both of her hands without opening her eyes. The tea always made her tired.

Kellen took one, and I took the other. Mother's thin fingers felt so frail in my own.

"I have been blessed with two beautiful, headstrong daughters who not only know how to care for themselves but for others, too. Your beauty is not in the texture of your skin or the shine of your hair. It's what's inside each of you, and it's how you influence the world around us. You are my sun, Eloise. And you, my moon, Kellen. Both lights shine brightly and fill my life with joy."

She gave our hands a gentle squeeze.

"You would fill my life with more joy if one of those thick-headed miscreants had caught your fancy, though."

She peeked at us from under the lashes of one eye before closing it again.

"I hardly believe a miscreant—"

"Or a band of them," Kellen added.

"—is what you had in mind for our future spouses," I said.

Mother sighed.

"Too right you are. A handsome man with a good heart and steadfast loyalty, like your father, is what I hope for both of you. Go now. I need to rest. Anne dosed my tea again. Tell her this concoction tasted like shite from the yard."

I choked on my laugh while Kellen shook her head.

While Mother rested, we took the tray to the kitchen.

"How is she today?" Judith asked.

"The same," Kellen said. "Dying."

"Aren't we all?" Judith said, not put out by Kellen's bluntness. "Some of us just take longer going about it and don't see it for what it is. The end comes for all of us, Kellen. It's what we do with the days we have that matters."

Kellen nodded and grabbed her cloak. I did the same. Side by side, we walked down the hill toward town. Just before the path met the larger road, we took a small walking trail to the right and started the trek up the rocky incline. Neither of us spoke until we reached the top. There, we stood near the edge and looked out over Towdown.

"Mother received a letter from Father yesterday. He's due to return soon," Kellen said.

Mother hated when Father had to leave. However, given his profession, he left often.

"I don't blame him," Kellen said when I didn't speak.

I turned to look at my sister.

"For staying away," she clarified even though I knew my sister well enough to guess most of her thoughts.

The world might see Kellen's steady, light blue gaze and bland expression as being unfeeling. But, I knew better. I saw her expression for what it was. A mask to hide the pain. It hurt her to see Mother like this...almost as much as it hurt Father.

Wrapping my arms around Kellen, I stared down at the rooftops and the lazy spirals of smoke hazing the air. The din from town didn't reach us, and the wind kept all but the barest hint of smoke from the air. Just beyond the rooftops, I could see the glimmer of white stone in the sun. The castle.

With a sigh, Kellen placed her head on my shoulder and wrapped her arms around my waist in return.

"Mother knows we all love her deeply. That's why she hired Anne," I said. "She hopes we will leave when the time is right."

"Since marriage appeals to you as little as it appeals to me, I doubt either of us is going anywhere," Kellen said. "Having Anne here hasn't changed that."

"Mother's hope will continue, regardless."

Kellen lifted her head and stepped away from me.

"What does the future hold for us?" she asked.

"Spinsterhood, most likely. Nothing too terrifying," I said.

The faint pounding of hooves drew our attention.

"We'd better get back," she said.

I followed her down the familiar trail. By the time we made it to the stable, Hugh had already unsaddled Sugar.

"Was there any trouble?" I asked.

"None. The hounds don't belong to hunters. They

belong to the Crown. It seems the Royal Retreat is due for a visit."

Kellen and I shared a look. I could barely recall the last time the rambling estate, a bit further up the hill, had been used. It had been at least five years ago. Neither Kellen nor I had gotten a glimpse of the royal entourage during the king's week-long visit then. We'd been strictly forbidden from leaving our small estate.

"We must tell Mother," Kellen said.

Judith was absent from the kitchen, but a small roast spit over the fire said she would return soon. I inhaled deeply.

"Stop smelling dinner, and tie your shoes," Kellen said without rancor.

"This is why you're four inches shorter. You don't appreciate your food, so you don't grow."

She snorted, and I knew I'd amused her even if her face didn't show it.

Anne was sitting quietly in the corner, reading from a primer, when we entered the parlor. She left us to wait for Mother to wake. It didn't take long for her to open her eyes and smile at us.

"Did you watch me sleep long?" she asked.

"Ages," I answered. "One doesn't often see a sleeping princess."

Her smile widened.

"Speaking of royalty," Kellen said. "It seems the hounds

belong to the king. He has finally decided to visit his Royal Retreat."

The Royal Retreat was more than just a massive stretch of land north of Towdown. It was also the name of the sprawling home the royal family used when they wanted some time away from the castle.

"This is not good news," Mother said, looking concerned. "It would be best if you stayed out of the woods while the king is in residence at the retreat."

Most mothers would be excited for a chance encounter with royalty, especially since we lived on royal land and were allowed to hunt it when others were not. Not our mother.

"I cannot imagine needing two homes," I said, trying to distract her from her worry. "It's not fun cleaning one."

"Do you honestly think His Highness cleans anything?" Kellen asked.

I grinned.

"Certainly his privy. It wouldn't be fair to ask someone else to do that."

Kellen nudged me with her elbow, and I realized what I'd said. Mother used nothing but a chamber pot that Anne, Kellen, or I cleaned every day.

"They would rob him blind," I added smoothly.

"How so?" Kellen asked.

"Come now. It's obvious." I paused for a moment and glanced between Mother and Kellen. "His shite is gold."

Mother burst out laughing, and Kellen shook her head.

"Eloise, I hope that you find your beau soon."

"Why is that, Mother?"

"Because you'll soon outswear him. A lady shouldn't speak so."

"Too right. But, any man worthy of my interest will need to take me as I am. Filthy mouth and all."

Anne knocked on the open door, calling our attention.

"There is a delivery boy," she said.

"Send him in," Mother said.

Anne disappeared, and a few moments later, a youth walked in. He was dressed in neat trousers and a coat that was just a tad too short for his wrists. A common sight for growing boys. His gaze swept over the three of us, and he removed the floppy red cap with a gold emblem on it from his shaggy dark head to give a precise, small bow.

"Can we help you?" Mother asked.

"Yes, ma'am. I have a delivery for Mrs. Cartwright." He lifted the small, brown paper-wrapped package he held.

"I am she," Mother said.

The boy came forward.

"A coin, Kellen," Mother said.

Kellen gave the boy a copper in exchange for the package. With a bob of his head, he returned to Anne, who I knew would see him out.

Mother smiled in excitement as Kellen handed her the package. The gifts that Father always sent made his absence less cruel. Each one let us know he was thinking of us.

"I should wait until he returns to open it," she said.

I grinned.

"At least, until yours arrive," she added. Her eyes never left the package.

"He sent yours ahead of his arrival for a reason," Kellen said. "Open it. We want to see what it is."

Mother didn't need any further encouragement. She tugged the string free and removed the paper to expose a small, cloth-covered box. We all gasped when she removed the lid to reveal a gold encased emerald pendant strung on a delicate gold chain.

"Your father's latest venture must have done very well," Mother said, breathlessly.

She lifted the chain and let the pendant dangle in the sunlight. It almost seemed to glow with a light of its own.

"It's beautiful," Kellen said.

"Help me put it on. I want your father to see me wearing it when he returns."

Kellen stood and helped Mother ease the chain over her hair then rearranged her braid prettily to lay over one shoulder.

"There," she said, moving back.

The sunlight, streaming in through the window, reflected against the stone; and an unnatural green light flashed in Mother's eyes briefly as she looked at me.

"What do you think?" she asked.

"You've never been more beautiful," Kellen said when I hesitated.

She smiled and blinked heavily.

"I believe this gift overexcited me. I need to rest for a bit."

She didn't rest, though. She exhaled loudly, her lids half closing.

"Mother?" I said, standing to touch her face. "Mother?"

She didn't respond.

"I don't think she's breathing, Eloise," Kellen said softly.

CHAPTER TWO

"ANNE!" I SCREAMED AS KELLEN PUT HER HEAD ON Mother's chest.

Anne came running into the room, her skirts lifted to her knees.

Kellen straightened, looking at the woman.

"I can't hear her heart beating."

A moment of silence gripped the room, and a heavy weight settled on my chest.

The expression on Anne's face shifted from fear to grief to a carefully composed mask. She went to Mother and set her head to chest for a moment before facing us.

"Your mother's gone," she said softly. "We all knew the tincture wouldn't work forever. Your mother, most of all. She asked me to give each of you a message when the time came."

She stepped close to Kellen and wrapped my sister in her arms.

"You are my moon. When you look at the stars, know that I'm watching you and love you always." Kellen didn't wrap her arms around Anne in return, but it didn't stop Anne from pressing a kiss to my sister's temple.

My throat ached when Anne released Kellen and looked at me.

I welcomed her hug, and her message from my mother.

"Take care of your sister," she whispered. "Your light will need to burn brightly for both of you in the days to come. Know that I love you. Always. Know that I am with you when the sun touches your skin, and hear me in every songbird's voice."

I hugged Anne in return.

"Thank you."

When she was done, she sent us from the room.

"Send Judith to me. We will care for Margaret."

Kellen and I didn't speak as we went to the kitchen. I didn't have the words necessary to break the numb state of disbelief that entombed my mind.

"Mother is gone," Kellen said calmly. "Anne will need your help bathing her."

Judith stared at us in shock for a moment before she went running.

Kellen went straight for the door, and I followed in her wake.

We found Hugh was in the stable, oiling the leather fastenings of the carriage.

"Mother is gone," Kellen said. "You will need to fetch a coffin. We will bury her the day after tomorrow."

Hugh removed his hat, his expression filled with sorrow.

"My condolences, Kellen. Eloise."

I nodded at him, took my sister's hand, and led her down the drive to the path we always took when we needed to escape, even just for a moment.

Neither Kellen nor I spoke until we reached the ridge.

"It wasn't time," Kellen said in a flat voice, her eyes dull.

I stared off in the direction of the castle, my mind still numbed with a reality it seemed unable to process. Mother was dead. Gone forever. She was the reason we both still lived at home. The reason we never entertained thoughts of marriage.

She'd been sick as long as I could remember. A weak constitution many a learned doctor had said. Yet, I'd thought she would live as long as any other because we cared for her so well. Kellen and I had both expected to care for her until our hair turned grey with age.

In a single moment, everything had changed.

"What will become of us now?" Kellen asked, almost as if reading my mind.

I wrapped my arm around her waist and held her as she set her head on my shoulder. I hurt more for the pain I knew she struggled to contain and thought of Anne's message from Mother. Kellen needed me to be strong.

THE FRONT DOOR SLAMMED. I jumped at the loud noise, and Kellen looked up in surprise from the needlepoint she was pretending to do.

Since we'd returned from the ridge the day before, a hush had stolen over the house. No sisterly banter. No echo of Mother's laughter. Nothing but sitting and waiting to lay Mother to rest. No one would call on us during the seven days the house was in deep mourning. We'd ensured our privacy to grieve by draping the front door with black, as was custom, to warn away callers. After seven days, the gossipmongers would start to arrive to offer their condolences and glean what information they could from our misery.

Feeling the spark of my temper ignite at the loud intrusion, I stood and went to the hall.

The sight of Father standing in the entry, shaking out his jacket stunned me. He turned to find me staring at him and smiled widely, his eyes lighting with joy.

"Eloise! There you are. Come see what I've brought you."

I stared at him in confusion at the very typical greeting. Surely he'd seen the black draping on the door.

"Father, did you not—"

Kellen's hand settled on my shoulder.

"Hello, Father," she said.

"Kellen, my heart. You look lovelier every time I return. I brought you something special. Just what you need."

He reached into his coat and withdrew two paper packages. Kellen's was a small square. Mine was long. At least the length of my forearm.

"Let's sit in the parlor so we can open them," he said.

Kellen's fingers twitched on my shoulder.

"Perhaps your study, Father," she said as he started toward us.

"Nonsense. The parlor is where you always open gifts."

I glanced at Kellen, unsure what to do.

"He's not ready," she said softly.

I stepped forward to intercept him.

"Father, there's something you should know about Mother."

He stopped to place a kiss on my cheek.

"She has died, Eloise. We have not. She would not like us to act like we did."

With a fatherly pat on my shoulder, he walked around me and entered the parlor.

On a higher level, I knew what he said was pure truth. Yet, his words fell like a hammer to my heart. A whisper of noise and twin intuition told me Kellen still stood just behind me.

"Remember, some are better at hiding what they truly feel."

I nodded and took her hand. We entered the parlor where Mother was laid out in her best gown. Father stood looking out the window, less than an arm's length from her. He didn't acknowledge her presence at all when he turned to look at us.

"Go on, then. Open them," he said, gesturing to the packages on our chairs.

I dutifully picked up the package and sat to wait for Kellen to open hers. I always made her go first.

She removed the string and opened the paper to reveal a silky, red ribbon.

"Thank you, Father. It's beautiful."

I opened my package to find a small, bareroot tree. There were no shoots coming from the single stem, but it did have a few nubs that promised branches in the future.

"A pear tree," Father said when I glanced up at him. "You had a sweet tooth when I was last home."

I smiled slightly, remembering how I'd tried to talk Judith into making sweet pastries.

"Thank you, Father. These gifts are lovely."

"As are the two of you."

He inhaled deeply and tucked his hands behind his back. It was a pose Kellen and I knew well. The pose he used to deliver news he knew we wouldn't like. Such as his departure.

"You are of an age now," he began. "Old enough to make your own decisions and to care for yourselves."

My stomach dropped to my toes as I feared that this wasn't a departure speech but a proposal discussion.

"I expect now that your mother has passed on, it won't be long before you're married and gone from this house," he continued, unaware how the callously delivered words twisted my stomach.

"That being the case, I see no reason to delay my next venture. I will leave tomorrow."

I couldn't decide if I was relieved he wasn't trying to marry us off or angry that he seemed barely affected by Mother's death. Until he'd mentioned it, I hadn't been sure he'd even noticed.

"We bury Mother tomorrow," Kellen said. "You cannot leave until after that."

"Of course. Of course. We should see her to her final resting place near dawn. She loved watching the sun come up." For a moment, something crept into his gaze. Something real and alive and in pain. With a flash, it was gone again.

"I will tell Hugh of our plans and see you at dinner." He strode from the room without a backward glance.

"If that is love," Kellen said, "I want no part in it. Ever."

I captured her hand in mine and waited for her to look at me. When she did, I saw her careful mask was slipping. Anger reflected in her gaze.

"We don't know what he's feeling right now. And what he felt for Mother is but one kind of love. Mother showed us another. Never forget hers. Or mine, Kellen."

She nodded and pulled away. I let her go, knowing she needed her space.

While she went to her room to regain an iron-fisted control over her emotions, I went to the kitchen. Judith and Anne were making pastries.

"Those look fancy," I said, dipping a finger in the lemon curd and earning a swat on my hand.

"They were fancy before you marked them."

I snorted and licked my finger.

"I only marked the one. Since it offends you, I'll remove it." Judith lifted her spoon menacingly as I reached again, and I laughed. It felt good. But it only lasted a moment before the pain crept back in.

Holding my hands up in surrender, I backed away from the table.

"Did Father return with the lemons?" They weren't a common item this side of the Dark Forest, but he was quick-witted with his trading.

"No. I bought them at market." Judith's humor fled as she wiped her hands on her apron and looked away from me. "Mrs. Cartwright was known by many even if she didn't leave the house. People will come to pay their respects, and we will have refreshments that will give the gossips something to talk about."

I hated the idea of opening our home to any visitors. Gossipmongers, all of them.

"If we offer them nothing, maybe they won't stay," I said.

Anne clucked her tongue.

"You're smarter than that, Eloise. That will be the first bit of information they'll slaver over." She assumed a gossipy pose and changed her voice. "'Can you believe those girls. They didn't offer us one bit of refreshment.'" She lowered her pitch to a snide whisper. "'Not surprised. With their father gone and their mother ill, they likely ran about like heathens.'"

"Your mother wouldn't tolerate that," Judith said. "Neither will I. She raised you well. Two fine young women who know how to be proper young ladies. Her one hope was that you'd both marry well. I won't let lack of refreshments dash her dreams."

No matter how much I wanted to deny it, I knew there was truth in her words. And, as greatly as I hated the idea of catering to the gossips, I couldn't allow them to say anything negative about Mother. Not now. Not ever.

"You're right. Can I help?"

"No. Go spend time with your father. You never know how much you'll have."

I nodded and left with my cloak. A sweep of the yard turned up no trace of Father or Hugh. I stood by the chickens, wondering where the pair might have gone when I heard a faint, muffled thump and scrape. Following the noise through the trees to the west, I spotted Hugh in a small clearing not far from the house.

Sweat glistened on his pale, white torso as he worked dirt and stone from the shallow pit forming in the ground.

I'd never seen him that unclothed before. But then, he'd never had to dig a grave for us. I swallowed hard and quietly turned away to leave him to his task.

Back at the house, I continued my search for Father and found him once again in the parlor, standing beside Mother. With his back to me, he stared out the window, and I took a moment to commit this instant to memory. It would be the last time I would ever see them together.

His once golden hair had lost much of its yellow at the sides, and new lines creased the corners of his eyes. He also looked a bit leaner than the last time I saw him. He'd always been a trim and fit man, not gaining girth around the middle like so many others his age. When he was here, he would carry Mother to and fro as needed. When he was away, he said he often loaded and unloaded merchandise. Better that he complete the tasks than pay someone else. It was his work ethic that influenced Kellen and me and why we willingly labored alongside those we employed, unlike many of the pampered girls of our means.

"Father," I said softly so as not to startle him. "I saw Hugh in the clearing to the west. It's a lovely spot."

"Yes. Lovely."

His tone indicated he wasn't in the room with me. His distance didn't bother me. In fact, I was quite used to conversing with someone who didn't want to talk.

"The morning sun will shine through the trees in winter, and a blanket of flowers will cover the ground in spring and summer. It will be pretty."

I sat and looked at Mother.

"She was looking forward to your return," I said.

He said nothing.

"She loved the necklace you sent her."

"Eh?" He turned to look at me.

"The necklace," I said, pointing. "It's very beautiful. Where did you find it?"

His gaze drifted to Mother. Not a single emotion crossed his features until his gaze landed on the necklace. Something flickered in his gaze, a pain so deep it hurt to witness. But it disappeared before he turned back to the window.

"Remove it," he said after a moment. "The dead need no ornaments. It will only incite thieves to disturb her grave."

"Yes, Father," I said softly, not bothering to refute his logic. A thief wouldn't know which graves might contain jewels until after they checked.

The moment my fingers touched the cold green stone, a bolt of heat seared my fingers. I gasped and released the jewel. The color swirled as it settled back on Mother's skin. I stared in horror and understanding. The glint I'd witnessed when Kellen put the necklace on Mother hadn't been a play of light. It'd been magic.

A sickening feeling settled into my stomach as I removed the necklace, avoiding the stone. I went to Father, my heart breaking with the possibility that he'd been so desperate to ease her suffering that he'd actually killed the woman I knew he loved very deeply.

Stepping in front of him, I held up the necklace and struggled not to cry.

"Why did you send this, Father? Why now?"

His gaze held mine for a long moment before going back to the trees behind me.

"I did not send it to your mother. Judith said that the last gift overtaxed her and warned me to send no more. If you will excuse me, there is much for me to do and very little time. I will see you at dinner."

He turned and strode from the room, leaving me with more questions than answers. I lifted the fine chain in my hand and studied the stone. If Father hadn't sent the necklace, who had?

I left the room and headed for the stairs. Kellen needed to know what had happened. Together, we could figure out who—

I stopped on the steps and looked down at the necklace. I couldn't tell Kellen. Ever. I knew how her mind worked and what she would think the moment I told her my suspicion that the necklace had killed Mother. Kellen had been the one to place the necklace around our mother's neck. And if Kellen knew the stone had ended Mother's life prematurely, she would never forgive herself.

My grip tightened on the chain as helplessness sparked anger.

As quietly as I could, I went to Mother's room and

placed the offending necklace in her box of jewelry. My mind raced as I stared blindly at her other baubles. Who would have cause enough to want her dead? The need to know consumed me. I needed to find that delivery boy. Or maybe not. Perhaps I could deduce who if I knew the why.

I left the room and wandered the house. Try as I might, I couldn't think of a single reason why anyone would want Mother dead. She was—had been—a kind person. In recent years, she no longer went to town because she wasn't able, so she'd never had the opportunity to offend anyone. And, those who chose to come see her had always been graciously welcomed and treated like a dear friend. There hadn't been many of those visits, either. Other than Judith and Anne, Mother had no dear friends. No family beyond us girls, either.

When Judith called me for dinner, Father and Kellen were already seated in the dining room. Candles lit the table, and a fire crackled in the fireplace.

As soon as I took my seat, Father gestured that we should begin eating. Since Mother's death, nothing appealed to me. But, I picked up my fork and took a bite, determined not to give Kellen any reason to suspect something was wrong.

After several silent minutes, Father spoke.

"We cannot undo what's been done. Our only option is to carry on and make the best of the circumstances in which we find ourselves. That was something your mother once said to me long ago. And she was right. That is why, tomorrow, I leave for my new venture. I know this won't be an easy time for you, and I'm sorry for that. I've made arrangements for someone to stay with you until I return."

"And how long will that be?" Kellen asked, her tone formal and indifferent. I knew better. She was angry.

"I'm not certain," he said.

I wasn't sure how I felt. I loved Father, and he had always put our needs before his own, working tirelessly to ensure we wanted for nothing. Yet, now when we most needed him to stay, he was set on leaving. His departure would surely be seen by the gossips as the abandonment it was. His disregard for Mother and us sparked my temper fiercely. Yet, if someone killed Mother, I would not ask him to stay. Without knowing who wanted Mother dead, I couldn't be certain Father wasn't also at risk. It was best that he was leaving.

"Where will this venture take you?" I asked, thinking that perhaps he might take us with him this time. It could be an adventure.

"To the kingdom of Turre."

My mouth dropped open.

"Surely you jest," I said. "That would take you through—"

"The Dark Forest. I know." He calmly took a bite of his roast.

I stared at him in shock, my thoughts colliding. Nothing good lived in the aptly named Dark Forest that ran from mountain range to mountain range, separating the kingdom of Drisdall from the kingdom of Turre. Kellen and I had grown up hearing tales of travelers who entered the dark depths never to return, and we listened to the faint, mournful howls on still nights.

"If you go, you will die," Kellen said, setting down her fork. "Is losing one parent not enough? Must we lose both?"

"Don't go, Father," I added. The possibility of a threat to his life if he remained was far better than the certainty of what he would face in the Dark Forest.

He sighed heavily.

"There is no need for such dramatic theatrics. You both know travelers passed through the Dark Forest at one time. I mean to establish a route again. Think of the trade possibilities. The riches. I heard rumor that the forest isn't as inhospitable as it once was. If that's true, it's more important than ever that I leave immediately. He who controls the route controls the trade."

Kellen looked down at her food, her cheeks flushed.

"Do not leave us, Father," I said again.

"My mind is set. I leave tomorrow after sunrise."

CHAPTER THREE

I HELD KELLEN'S HAND AS HUGH SHOVELED DIRT OVER Mother's coffin. Father stood at the head of her grave where a wooden marker now stood. A weak orange light filtered in through the trees and painted the clear blue sky. It was a beautiful day. A beautiful, terrible, heartbreaking day.

When Hugh finished, he nodded to us and left quietly.

Father hadn't said anything when he'd joined us outside and said nothing still. He stared down at the fresh earthy mound, once again closed off.

Kellen gave my hand a light squeeze and walked away. I was grateful she'd left before Father. At some point during my restless night, I'd decided to tell him about the necklace. It was something I should have done in the first place. I'd been too shocked to think clearly the day before, though.

"Father, there's something you should know."

He looked up at me.

"I believe the necklace killed Mother. Her eyes glowed the moment it settled around her neck. I thought it was a trick of the light, but when I touched it yesterday, I felt something. Magic, I think."

Father stepped toward me and grabbed my arms, his grip bruising.

"Say nothing of your suspicions ever again. Do you understand? To do so will mean your death."

"But—"

My father, who doted on Mother, Kellen, and me, and never spoke a harsh word, shook me firmly. I stared up at him in shock until I noted fear in his eyes. Fear for me. Fear for what even a whispered word of something so forbidden could do.

"Yes, Father," I said softly.

He released me with an unsteady exhale.

"Very good. Will you walk with me to the house?"

We traversed the path in silence, and when we rounded the house, I saw a horse saddled and waiting. Kellen stood on the front step, her expression closed off to what she was feeling.

"You're leaving already?" I asked, noting Father's red merchant jacket waiting atop the saddle.

"As I said I would."

"But, I thought once I told you—"

He gave me a sharp look.

"You are smart and resourceful girls. Keep your wits.

Take care of one another. Mind the rules. You'll both be fine."

He agilely swung himself up onto the horse's back and removed something resting at the front of his saddle.

He handed me the bare branch he'd given me as a gift the day before.

"Don't forget to plant this. Farewell, my daughters."

Without any words of comfort, he prodded the horse forward.

Kellen turned on her heel and went into the house. I couldn't go inside. My mind was too full of grief, anger, and excessive questions to which I had no answers.

Instead, I ran back to my mother's grave and fell to my knees. I wished I could bury my feelings like Kellen. To suppress the hurt. But I couldn't. It boiled out of me in a torrent of tears.

I didn't understand Father's refusal to stay. Did he truly grieve so deeply that he couldn't see how desperately Kellen and I needed him?

If it was truly magic that had killed Mother what were Kellen and I to do? No. What was I to do? For the first time in my life, I felt completely alone.

It took some time for the tears to slow. When they did, the sun was peeking over the trees, and the soft chitter of animals had come alive around me. Wiping my face dry, I looked at my mother's grave. Time would flatten the mound of dirt. Plants would grow and disguise that a grave had ever existed. Only the marker would stand tall. But for how long? Maybe twenty years before it needed to be replaced? I dug a hole in the soft soil over her casket and planted the pear shoot.

Sitting back on my heels, I looked at the tiny thing.

"It's not much now," I said softly. "But someday, in spring, dainty white petals will rain down on your head. Their fragrance will perfume the air, and songbirds will sit in the branches. Their sweet melody will keep you company even if I'm not here."

My words caught, and I started to cry again.

A rustle and grunt from the nearby trees sent me to my feet, ready to bolt. Wild boar were wickedly dangerous.

"You stupid beast, walk faster or I'll see you on a plate."

An old woman with bits of twigs sticking out of her tangled nest of white hair tumbled out of the thicket. The worn and patched brown cloak that hung from her shoulders had seen better days. So had her dress. In her fist, she held one end of a rope on which she tugged mightily. An enormous pig reluctantly waddled into the clearing behind her.

I'd never seen such a well-fed beast. He was easily twice the size of the woman, and he didn't waddle with disdain but with strain. I didn't see how his small legs could support his body.

By appearances, they must have come from an outlying farm.

When the woman noticed me, she stopped tugging on the pig and gave me a pleasant smile.

"Good morning," she said. "I thought I heard someone out here. Could you be so kind as to tell me where 'here' is?"

Her lightly accented words told me she was from much further north.

"You are near Towdown. It's just over the next rise." I pointed to the south.

"Towdown," the woman said with distaste. "Not a place I wanted to visit. I've heard that magic has been banned here. Is that true?"

"Yes," I said nervously. As Father had recently reminded me, no one should speak openly of magic.

"Where were you hoping to be?" I asked, changing the subject.

"Adele preferably."

"Adele? I've never heard of that town."

The old woman considered me for a moment.

"Town? Never heard of it? Strange child. Everyone has heard of the city of Adele and its white towers. It's the best market for fine silks and fresh citrus."

I shrugged apologetically.

"I'm sorry. I don't often venture from my home, and when I do, it's only to visit Towdown's market."

She waved away my apology.

"It's no matter. I know where I am now and that I need to head west."

"Head west? You don't want to do that. There's nothing to the west but the Dark Forest." My gaze flicked to the pig.

"You'll never make it through that cursed place with such a tasty treat for the beasts."

She gave the pig a satisfied smile.

"Do you hear that, pig? We can go through the Dark Forest, and I can watch you be eaten. Seems a fitting end for you."

The pig made a squealing sound almost as if he understood her.

Her smile faded as she cocked her head and studied me for a long quiet moment.

"I'm not sure what to think of you."

"Think of me?" I asked, careful to keep any hint of judgement from my tone.

I looked down at my skirt and saw where the material was stained with dirt from kneeling. I brushed as much as I could away before looking up again. Her gaze flicked to the mounded dirt at my feet.

"Who was that?" she asked.

"My mother."

"Was she a good woman?"

The blunt question surprised me.

"She was a very good woman," I said. "Her name was Margaret Cartwright."

"You sure you want to plant that tree there?" she asked.

"Yes. The marker will weather and rot long before a pear tree will."

She made a non-committal noise.

"What is your name?" she asked.

"Eloise."

"Do you practice magic?"

This woman was dangerous in her ignorance.

"No," I said emphatically. "I think it best that I go now."

"I must beg a favor, Eloise," she said, stopping me from leaving. "I'm old and tired, and this pig moves slower than me. I have places I must be and have no time to wait for him. If I leave him in your care, will you eat him?"

I looked at the pig, who stared back at me. I wasn't opposed to caring for animals, but I wasn't so sure about this one. Something in his eyes seemed to plead with me, an almost human quality that made me want to shiver and politely refuse her. However, I couldn't. I'd witnessed her struggle with the beast.

"No, ma'am. I will not eat him."

The woman started forward, tugging the pig along.

"Then I will leave him in your care for a while. I have nothing to offer you for his keep, though."

"There is no need. I like animals and won't mind caring for another one. It will be a welcome distraction."

I glanced at my mother's grave, feeling the sharp stab of grief anew.

The old woman caught my hand in her own. Turning it over, she studied my palm then glanced at the grave. Was she checking if I was dirty? When she looked up, she captured my gaze with a shrewdness that contradicted her age.

"I wasn't expecting this," she said softly.

"I beg your pardon?"

"Never mind me." She shook her head slightly. "Distractions are good when grieving, but don't forget these rules. Feed him lightly but once a day. He has been overindulged his whole life. If he continues to be over indulged, he will certainly die a horrible death. Do not trust him. He is an animal who would sacrifice you to gain his freedom. Walk him through the forest twice a week. You never know what he will find for you. He knows how to earn his keep."

She pressed the rope into my hand.

"If you need me, you can ask for Rose at the Brazen Belle in Towdown."

"I thought you were headed to Adele."

"I am. But, I believe there is business here that I must address first." She started past me, her stride surprisingly agile for her age.

"Take care, Eloise, and mind the pig."

As soon as she disappeared, the pig started nosing the base of my skirts.

"None of that, now," I said. "If you misbehave with me, Hugh will take over your care. And, Hugh does not care for pigs."

The pig grunted and followed me willingly enough as I started toward the house. I decided not to notice how he was more docile with me than he had been with the old woman. Or the way he kept glancing at me. Instead, I focused on the encounter with the old woman. Rose.

Why would she ask if I practiced magic? As my father had warned me, it was dangerous to even utter the words, ignorant or not. But more than that, why would she ask it of me only hours after burying my mother whom I suspected had been killed by magic?

After tucking the pig into the vacant pig pen, I fetched water from the well and quickly washed my hands and face before going inside. Neither Judith nor Anne were in the kitchen.

While I nibbled on a bit of roast I'd found set aside for me, I considered the circumstance in which Kellen and I found ourselves. The expectations we'd once held for our future, to care for our ailing parent, had drastically changed. We could no longer hide away at the estate like we had. We were of an age where most girls were either betrothed or already wed. Although Mother had wanted the same for us, I knew the next trip to the market wasn't going to undo the impressions that had already been made.

Thankfully, the need to follow society's expectations to find a suitor would need to wait. Propriety demanded seven days of full-mourning. After that, a minimum of thirty days of half-mourning.

Kellen and I had four more days of peace.

"THAT'S ALL YOU GET," I said when the pig looked up at me. "The old woman is right. You'll die if I continue to overfeed you. Remember, pigs who still need fattening avoid the butcher's block."

The rattle of a carriage drew me away from the pig's pen and his displeased grunts. Instead of passing by, the sound seemed to draw closer. I moved to the house and paused on the steps, waiting to see who it might be. Behind me, a swath of black material hung from the door, an obvious reminder that we were a house in full-mourning.

I hoped it wasn't an over-eager gossipmonger. Whatever shred of patience I'd possessed for snooping people no longer existed.

A carriage rolled up the drive. Nondescript, it certainly looked like the type easily rented from a smith in town. I watched the contraption slow to a stop as the driver nodded down to me. Before he could move from his perch, the door to the carriage flew open, and a woman garbed in black stepped down without assistance. The laced veil obscured her identity only a moment before she flipped it back.

Her black hair stunned me as much as her face. With her soft brown eyes, dark hair, and pale skin, she looked just like Mother.

"Eloise, my darling." She came toward me, a smile on her lips while tears gathered in her eyes. "I'm so sorry." She wrapped me in her arms and held me tightly to her bosom while her hand smoothed over my hair.

Comfort enveloped me, and I hadn't realized how

desperately I'd needed it. I only wished it was from someone I knew.

"Thank you," I said, hesitantly returning the hug. When she pulled back and gave me another tearful smile, I couldn't stop myself from asking, "Who are you?"

"Of course, Margaret wouldn't have mentioned an estranged cousin from her mother's side. How silly of me not to introduce myself. Call me Maeve. Consider me your fairy godmother. I'm here to set the world to rights."

She hooked her arm through mine and led me toward the house.

"When I heard your father planned to leave immediately, I offered to stay with you and Kellen. The two of you shouldn't face what's to come alone."

"Father mentioned making arrangements for someone to stay with us."

She stopped walking and looked at me with concern.

"He didn't tell you who?"

"No, ma'am."

She waved a hand in the air, a dismissive gesture Mother had often used.

"None of this ma'am nonsense. Call me Maeve or Auntie Maeve, if you prefer. I cannot believe that father of yours." She clucked her tongue and carefully removed her veil. "That's men for you, though. They don't deal well with grief and can't think clearly."

I opened my mouth to ask...well, anything, but a scrape of noise from the stairs drew our attention. I looked up to see Kellen, paler than usual, standing on the first landing. She was staring at Maeve. Given Maeve's resemblance to Mother, I understood her shock.

"Kellen, this is Maeve. She's here to help as Father mentioned."

Kellen blinked then nodded to Maeve.

"Welcome, Lady Maeve."

"Please call me Maeve or Auntie Maeve. There's no need for me to be Lady Grimmoire here. At least, not yet." She exhaled heavily and glanced at me. "We still have a few days of solitude before chaos descends, do we not?"

"Yes. Three more days."

"Very good. It will give us time to plan and prepare. But, that can wait for now. Is there somewhere I might rest for a bit?" she asked, looking between us. "Traveling always tires me."

Kellen and I shared a look. On the second floor, there were four bedrooms. Kellen and I shared the largest. Father had the smallest one, and Mother had the room with the nursery attached. With Mother gone, Anne had started sleeping downstairs with Judith in the room just off the kitchen. While Father's room was now also empty, we couldn't ask Maeve to sleep there. It would be highly improper, especially with visitors expected within days.

"I'll show you the way," Kellen said to Maeve.

I followed behind the pair as Kellen led her to Mother's room, Kellen having come to the same conclusion as I.

Maeve took one look at the room and shook her head.

"I cannot stay here. Is there an open servant's room? Even a mat in your attic would be welcome."

I looked around the beautifully furnished room in confusion.

"I'm sorry," I said. "This is all we have at the moment. You don't like it?"

Maeve caught me up in another hug.

"Dear child, this is your mother's room. Of course it's perfect." She pulled back and looked me in the eyes. "But, I'm here to ease your transition into a new life. To be your confidante and friend until you no longer need one. I'm not here to replace your mother or your memories of her. And, the last thing I want is for you to feel any animosity toward me. That wouldn't help any of us do what needs to be done. I fear that staying in this room would hinder our goals, not help them."

"We insist," Kellen said. "If you'd prefer not to sleep in this bed, there's another in the nursery that Anne used."

"We don't mind if you stay in here," I said. "There really isn't anywhere else."

Maeve gave us both searching looks and went to check the nursery.

"This does look comfortable. Are you sure you don't mind if I stay in this part?"

"Not at all," Kellen said.

"Perhaps after I rest, we can talk more, and you can introduce me to Anne."

THE WIND RATTLED the window near my head as I lay in bed. It was the only sound, beyond Kellen's steady breathing, that I could hear in the now quiet house. I rolled to my side and studied my sister's pale face in the weak moonlight.

"What do you think of her?" I asked quietly, seeing Kellen didn't yet sleep.

"She seems nice."

"She does. And Judith and Anne like her."

After waking from a long nap, Maeve had eaten lunch with us and then insisted on meeting our staff. She was cordial and friendly. Not what one would expect from someone who held the title of Lady Grimmoire.

"I was a bit surprised she wanted to see the pig," I said.

Kellen smiled in the dark.

"She didn't get too close, though, did she?"

I laughed. "No, she didn't. But that's okay. I don't think Mother would have gotten close, either."

We both grew quiet. It was nice having Maeve with us. It distracted us from the change in our routine since now there was no one to read to. No one to play for. No rhythm to our days without Mother's presence.

"It's childish, I know, but I don't want to like her," I said. "I know how I feel about her won't change what happened. Mother's gone. Yet, it feels wrong to like Maeve so quickly."

"Perhaps it's best to maintain your distance. Maeve is

here for a purpose, and once that purpose is fulfilled, she'll leave."

I knew what Kellen was thinking. Maeve would leave like Mother and Father.

"I won't leave you," I said.

"People always leave, Eloise. It's in our nature...how we're made. If not through abandonment, then by death."

"Well then, I will never abandon you. Ever."

Her eyes softened before she closed them.

"I believe you," she whispered.

CHAPTER FOUR

THE SOFT MURMUR OF VOICES DREW ME TO THE HALL WHERE Maeve and Kellen stood, looking into Father's room.

"Good morning," I said.

Maeve turned and smiled at me.

"Good morning, Eloise. I'm sorry if we disturbed you."

"Not at all." I glanced at Father's room then Kellen, who was usually never up this early. "Is everything all right?"

Maeve gave me a troubled look.

"Since your father anticipates his latest endeavor to take some time, I arranged for everything I hold dear to arrive within a fortnight. Kellen and I were discussing if there might be a way to accommodate what will arrive."

I joined them at Father's door. His room was very crowded and removing all but his bed would likely free much of the space. However, clearing his room would feel like we were giving up on his return.

"He never mentioned how long he planned to be gone,"
I said.

"That's odd. He told me at least four months."

The news felt like a slap.

Maeve's expression softened.

"The sun has barely risen. Far too early for this
conversation. Let us eat first. After, we can discuss my place
here."

Kellen and I followed Maeve to the dining room where
she started to take a seat.

"We eat in the kitchen in the morning," Kellen said. "It
makes—made things easier for Judith."

"Of course," Maeve said, immediately changing
course.

She followed us into the kitchen and greeted Judith and
Anne as we sat at the table. She accepted her soft-boiled
egg and didn't say anything when the pair joined us. I was
very grateful for that. Anne and Judith were a part of our
family. Hugh, too, though he preferred to eat earlier than
the rest of us. Kellen and I had just lost our parents, and I
refused to bend to social etiquette and distance myself
from any of them.

After we finished our soft-boiled eggs, it didn't surprise
me when Maeve once again brought up the problem of
where to store her possessions.

"Mother's room makes the most sense," Kellen said.
"We live in a modest home and need to be practical with
how we use the space we have. Moving Mother's

possessions to the attic is reasonable as Father might come back to us while Mother never will."

Maeve studied Kellen for a moment then reached out to put her hand over my sister's. However, Kellen moved her hand from the table before Maeve could touch her.

"Would you be interested in going to the market with me today, Lady Grimmoire?" Anne asked, smoothly deflecting the moment. "Judith can help the girls move Mrs. Cartwright's things to the attic while we're gone."

"I hate the idea of leaving all the work to the three of them," Maeve said, a light of impending protest in her eyes.

"As you've said, we have only a few days until visitors start arriving. A trip to the market is necessary and one Eloise and I cannot perform during our mourning period," Kellen said. "It makes sense to divide our numbers to complete what must be done in a short period of time."

Maeve inclined her head. "You are very sensible, Kellen. That will help you greatly in the days ahead."

I breathed a silent sigh of relief that Maeve wasn't put out by Kellen's manner. While Anne went to tell Hugh to hitch the wagon, Maeve accompanied us upstairs.

"Do not strain yourselves moving anything heavy," she warned. "Hugh can assist with those things when we return."

"We will be careful," I promised as my gaze wandered over Mother's things.

After Maeve left, it didn't take Kellen, Judith, and me long to dismantle and move the bed upstairs. Carrying the smaller pieces of furniture to the attic was a bit more tedious and required many trips.

Having returned for the next piece, a chair near the window, I paused to stare at the plain wooden box that contained every item Father had ever brought home for Mother. The green necklace was no longer there. It had never belonged with her treasured items. Instead, I'd hidden it under a board in our room before Maeve arrived.

Despite Father's warning, I couldn't put thoughts of the necklace out of my mind. Something had happened when I'd touched the pendant just as certainly as something had happened to Mother when Kellen had put it on her.

Although I knew Father's admonition to keep silent had been to protect me, I couldn't help my resentment that he'd done nothing after hearing my suspicions. Surely, he couldn't be agreeable with someone killing his wife? Perhaps that was the reason behind his determination to leave so quickly. If he had stayed and brought to light that someone had used magic on the king's own land, what would have happened? I swallowed hard. Father's death. Perhaps ours, too.

I should follow his example and put what happened behind me. Yet words lingered in my mind, haunting me with their insistence. Who? Why? Would I never know the answers?

Kellen walked into the room and caught me looking at Mother's jewelry box.

"Perhaps we should move the jewelry box to our room instead of the attic," she said.

"No, I don't think I can wear any of her treasures just yet. And seeing the box would only bring pain right now."

She nodded and didn't question me when I carried it out of the room.

The attic, already full of so many castoffs, was now crowded with the addition of Mother's furniture. There was still room to walk between pieces and find a safe place for the box in a back corner, though.

By midday, Mother's room was cleared, and Anne and Maeve had returned. We ate a companionable lunch in the kitchen then moved to the sitting room while Hugh moved the last pieces of furniture into the attic.

"Anne was quite informative today," Maeve said.

"Informative?" I asked.

"Yes. About who might be visiting and with whom I needed to have the most care."

"I'm not sure I understand," I said.

"The gossips," Maeve said bluntly. "Those who will come to give condolences but are really only here to gain information to share with their friends over tea."

"That would be every woman who passes over our threshold tomorrow," Kellen said.

"Not the men?" Maeve asked.

"Father had many business contacts. The men who call will likely only be here as a show of respect and will not linger long."

"I see," Maeve said. She glanced at me, but I couldn't contradict Kellen's assessment.

"Well, that does make me question how much effort and funds to put into refreshments."

"Unfortunately, no matter how much we dislike those who attend, we cannot slight our responsibilities," Kellen said. "To do so would reflect poorly on our love for our mother."

"You are quite right," Maeve said. "Then, there is only one other matter to discuss. Do you want to be present? If so, both of you will need to acquire the appropriate attire."

I looked down at my hands, dreading what she meant. The black gowns of mourning. Everywhere we went, people would know our grief. We wouldn't be able to escape it. Not even for a moment.

"I would prefer to mourn in solitude," Kellen said, saving me from trying to come up with a diplomatic answer.

"I agree," I said.

"Very well. I will welcome and speak to every guest on your behalves. Is there anything you wish me to say to them?"

"'Go away' has a nice ring to it," I said.

Maeve chuckled. "If only it were that easy."

"Thank them for coming to share our grief and offering their support in our time of need," Kellen said.

My sister always seemed to have the right words to say.

But, I knew what she was thinking on the inside as her thoughts often echoed my own.

THE PIG TUGGED ME ALONG, content to root about the forest for whatever he smelled. Thanks to his nose, I had two dark mushrooms in my pocket. Judith would know what to do with them.

"Come, Mr. Pig," I said. "It's time for us to return home."

He stopped his rooting and looked up at me. I disliked the way it sometimes seemed as if he was thinking. Pigs didn't think. They couldn't. If I ever let myself believe they did, I'd never be able to eat bacon again.

A thud echoed through the barren trees, quickly followed by another. Frowning, I started toward the noise, glad for a reason not to return home. While spring was still struggling to make its presence known with gusty, cool winds, here in the shelter of the estate's forest, the breeze was mild and the temperature almost pleasant. Walking amongst the trees was much preferable to being shut in the house for another day.

The pig, however, didn't seem to be of the same mind. Before I took more than a few steps, he balked, tugging the rope from my hand.

"Go then. I'm sure some hunter would enjoy spotting you alone in the woods."

He let out a loud squeal, and I quickly shushed him.

"We don't know who is ahead. You're not the only one who might be accosted by wayward hunters." I picked up the rope. "Your silence might earn you an extra handful of grain when we return."

When he remained silent, I started forward again, weaving my way through the trees to find the source of the continuous sound. When we reached the tall oak that marked the boundary of our small estate, I hesitated. I knew very well what lay ahead and who I might find. Well, not who exactly.

My curiosity getting the better of me, I continued north. It didn't take long before I spotted a man through the trees.

Like when Hugh labored with the earth, this man wore no shirt while laboring to cut wood. Unlike Hugh, this man's back wasn't pale. It was golden and rippled in a captivating fashion with each swing of his ax.

"Stay here," I said absently to the pig, needing to move closer.

I crept forward on silent feet, watching the man work. Steam rose off of his torso, and his skin glistened in the early morning light. Though I wasn't close enough to see any detail in his features, my pulse sped with appreciation of what I could see. He had a handsome form to be sure.

If this was an example of the king's men, I hoped the king was prepared to stay at the Royal Retreat a good long while.

The man stopped suddenly and grabbed his shirt from

a nearby log, wiping the sweat from his face. I waited in anticipation for him to turn, but he did not. Instead, he threw his shirt aside and reached for a water skin. When he tipped his head back to drink, the sunlight caught on his brown hair, turning it bronze.

My fingers twitched against the bark of the tree that hid me. What would he do if I stepped out and introduced myself? Probably think me wanton. Better to wait for him to be fully clothed.

Smiling to myself, I carefully backed away and almost tripped on the pig. Only nimble reflexes saved me from a fall and an awkward explanation. Scowling at the pig, I picked up his rope and quietly made my way back to the estate border.

My thoughts lingered on the man and his muscled torso. The moment that he swung and sun dappled his back, highlighting every ridge, repeated over and over in my mind. My cheeks warmed. Never before had I been so affected by a man. I knew a pretty face could hide an unsuitable character. *But it wasn't his face that had your heart racing*, I thought, my wistful smile returning.

The pig grunted and bumped into me.

"What?" I didn't like the way he was knowingly looking at me. "Who I look at is none of your concern. Now, do you want your grain or not?"

I gave the rope a tug, and he meekly followed me back to the house where I fed him a small portion of grain in his pen.

"Eloise," Kellen said from just behind me, making me jump.

When I turned to scowl at her, I caught the lingering hint of amusement.

"Are you here to startle me, or do you have a purpose?"

"A purpose. The first guest of the day has arrived. Would you like to go for a walk?"

In the three days since Maeve had entered our lives, Kellen and I had settled into an awkward routine. The awkwardness was due to our struggle to contrive tasks to keep ourselves occupied. Reading aloud without Mother there to listen seemed pointless and sad. The same with playing the piano. So Kellen and I found small things to do. I took care of the animals, which required very little of my time. And, Kellen organized the attic. When those tasks grew wearisome, we visited Mother's grave.

"A walk sounds nice," I said, dusting my hands off on my apron.

We gave the house wide berth and slipped into the trees. My thoughts went to the man in the woods, and I briefly considered sharing the story with Kellen. However, given the reason behind this second walk, I decided to save the tale for later.

"Who is the first visitor?" I asked instead.

"I'm not certain. I slipped out through the kitchen and avoided the introductions. Some Lady or someone from a House of something or other."

"Probably here for the lemon tarts," I said. Judith made

the best sweets. My mouth watered just thinking of the pastries that waited in cold storage

"Judith was counting the pastries this morning."

I grinned. Kellen knew I'd snuck down there yesterday to snitch one.

"Did she say anything?"

"Only that you were going to get fat."

I laughed.

My humor faded, however, when we reached the clearing, and I saw Mother's grave. Since her death, there were moments where I'd forget that Kellen and I were alone in the world. Then, some jarring reminder would shatter that fragile peace. It felt like the grieving would never end.

Kellen and I sat on the wooden bench that Hugh had placed there for us.

As I stared at the mound of dirt, I wished Mother was still with us. That Father was away on a normal business trip. And that Maeve, no matter how kind she was, wasn't living with us. In essence, I wanted the safety and ignorance of my old life to return.

The birdsong in the trees grew louder, and I thought of Mother's message to me. I tried to remind myself she was still with us in spirit, but it was too hard to hold such an unproven belief.

"It seems like it grew two inches overnight," Kellen said, jarring me from my thoughts.

"What has?"

Even as I asked, my gaze went to the pear tree. It remained nothing more than a single twig jutting from the ground, but Kellen was right. It did appear taller. I got up to look at the sapling closer and noted the buds were bigger as well.

"I'm glad it seems to be growing. It's like a piece of Father is here to watch over her, don't you think?"

I turned in time to catch Kellen's angry expression before she closed herself off again.

"There's no purpose in holding your anger," I said. "He's gone, and so is she. We cannot change how things are; we can only choose to accept them and move on."

"Move on," she said. "For what? A marriage to a man who will leave us just as readily as Father did?"

I returned to Kellen and set my head on her shoulder.

"Who said anything about us marrying some soddy men? We can make our own futures, can we not? Perhaps we should travel? We can pose as spinsters and see what lies to the north."

Kellen snorted, amused by my daydream. She set her head against mine.

"Let me hold my anger for a little while," she said. "I do so on Mother's behalf for she was never angry with Father a day in her life. And she should have been. At least twice."

"Twice?"

"The day he missed our birth and the day he missed her death. It's warranted."

My chest tightened, and my throat closed for a moment

as I struggled with my own pain. When I finally spoke, my voice was soft.

"It's a fair request. However, you've already carried your anger for seven days. I think that's sufficient. It's time to let it go."

She sighed.

"If I let it go, I have nothing left to do with myself. I miss her terribly."

"Me, too. Perhaps it's time we decided on new hobbies. Or we could always attend a gathering or two. Become renowned gossips. Think of all the cakes we could eat."

Kellen snorted again.

"Tomorrow I'll go to town and see what new books I can find."

The bookstore was a safe distance from the market, which meant it was a haven for Kellen.

"Books instead of cakes?" I said. "It's like I don't even know you, sister."

"You know me better than anyone. Would you like me to find a book for you, or will you come with me?"

"I'll be at your side, of course. Those boorish boys in the market aren't to be trusted, and my aim is far better than yours."

She chuckled then quieted. We sat like that for a long time, both lost in our own thoughts, before hunger drove us back to the house. Judith had a simple midday meal prepared for us when we arrived.

While we ate, Judith and Anne worked quietly. Their

lack of conversation made it painfully obvious someone still remained in the sitting room with Maeve. I wondered if it was the same person who had arrived earlier but didn't ask. It didn't matter who was here, only why they were here.

After lunch, Kellen and I went upstairs. Kellen entered Father's room to look over his collection of books to see if there was anything that might interest her. She'd never intruded on his space before. That she did so now could only mean she thought he wasn't coming back.

Leaving her to her quiet, I lay on my bed and pondered her questions of what was next for us. For all of my silly play about traveling, I wasn't yet ready to leave Towdown. There were questions that needed answers. Questions I'd tried to ignore but knew I couldn't. I needed to find the person responsible for robbing us of our family. I needed to know who had sent the necklace.

But not yet. First, I needed Kellen to choose her path in life. I needed to know she would be safe from any repercussions. Then, I could choose my own way and damn the consequences.

Sitting up, I checked the hall then carefully closed the door before kneeling at the end of my bed. I folded back the rug and pried up the floor board. It was a space I'd discovered many years ago. It had never held anything of importance because everything I had, I willingly shared with Kellen and Mother.

However, it had been the perfect place to keep the

necklace. A safe place so no one would touch it and suffer the same fate as Mother.

Carefully reaching in, I unfolded the soft leather in which I'd wrapped the pendant.

The necklace was gone.

CHAPTER FIVE

I KNELT THERE AND STARED AT THE HIDEY-HOLE IN confusion. How could the necklace be missing?

Grabbing the empty piece of leather, I replaced the board and righted the rug. The necklace didn't disappear on its own. I left the room and found Kellen still in Father's bedroom, looking at his meager collection of fictional stories amidst his accounting books.

She looked up as I entered.

"Unless I'm interested in reading the history of our accumulated wealth, or lack thereof, I'm afraid there isn't much here for me."

I closed the door so no one would overhear us.

"Please tell me you're not wearing it," I said in a hushed tone.

She frowned at me, her confusion clear.

"Wearing what?"

"The necklace. The green one that arrived for Mother. I had it in the hiding spot in the floor, and it's gone." I held out the empty piece of leather as proof.

"I didn't take it." She glanced at the leather then met my gaze. "Why did you hide it away if you didn't want any of Mother's jewelry as a reminder?"

There was no censure. Only my sister trying to understand my motivations.

"I didn't want the reminder." I sighed. "It's hard to explain. It was the last thing she received. It just felt important and private."

I couldn't lie to my sister. I never could. That was why all of what I said was true; yet, none of it came close to the truth.

"I understand," Kellen said. "Let's ask Judith and Anne."

However, Judith and Anne hadn't seen the necklace while tidying our room.

"You know how things are here," Judith said. "You can hear mice scratching in the walls at night. If you put a trinket in your hidey-hole, there's a chance that a mouse might have taken off with it. They like shiny things. We need a cat."

I knew she was right. Not about the cat but about the mice. The necklace wasn't the first item to go missing because of the cute pests. But, it was by far the most important. I should have known not to tempt fate by putting the necklace in the floor.

Angry with my own foolishness, I left the house alone. The wind tugged at my cloak as I walked toward Mother's grave. Having already visited with her today, I didn't stop again. Instead, I carried on through the trees, wandering the familiar woods.

Animals skittered through the underbrush, making way for my passing. Some scolded me with their little, outraged chitters. Normally, I would have been amused and paused to talk back to them. But, I couldn't. Not today. I was too angry.

How could I have been so careless? That necklace had been my one piece of proof that my mother hadn't died of a natural cause. Without it, the person responsible would never be brought to justice. Proof, when dealing with magic, was the key. Even with proof, things might have ended badly for me. However, without proof, my quest to find answers was over before it ever began.

I kicked at a fallen branch.

No, I couldn't think like that. The necklace wasn't gone forever. Just misplaced. If there were vermin in the house, they had to have a nest somewhere. I only needed to find it.

I was so lost in thought that the sudden, loud voice just in front of me took me by surprise.

"Leave now, by order of the king."

Startled, I jumped back as I looked up. My heel slipped,

and I tumbled backward. Time slowed as our gazes locked. Though I hadn't glimpsed his face earlier, I recognized the man.

The dark blue eyes of the nap-headed scoundrel held mine. He had the audacity to smirk as I landed with a soft splat on the spring-dampened ground. A cold moisture seeped through my skirts and chilled my backside.

Stunned, I stared up at the man as he leaned on his walking stick. Close to my age, he was far more handsome than he had a right to be. His broad shoulders were properly covered by a rough coat this time, but my pulse nevertheless skipped a beat as I recalled how he looked without it. However, since I wasn't sure if his humor was meant to be shared or at my expense, I refused to give my attraction to the man any due.

"Did you intend to send me flying into the mud?" I asked.

"I find that's where most of your kind belong."

My mouth dropped open, and my already frayed temper ignited. He was just like all the other pretty faces in town.

"You are a boorish ass," I said, setting my hands on the ground to hoist myself up. I ignored the squish of mud between my fingers and the surprised lift to his brows.

"Boorish ass?"

"Yes. Are you hard of hearing?"

I struggled to my feet, regretting that I hadn't noted the wet ground before my fall. His smirk widened with growing amusement each time I slipped and dirtied myself further. When I finally won my footing back with no offer of help from him, I was ready to throw a rock at his head. I could already imagine the hollow sound it would make when it connected.

"I do suppose braying ass would suit you better," I said with deceptive calm as I shook as much mud as I could from my skirts.

His humor fled, and he frowned at me.

"You have no right to call me anything," he said, once again sounding high-handed. "I am not the one trespassing."

How ridiculously presumptuous of him. This time, it was I who wore the smirk.

"Are you sure about that? This is the king's land. While I indeed have permission to be here, I doubt you do. It would be in your best interest to flee before I summon the king's guard."

He tilted his head to consider me. The vivid blue of his eyes held me for a moment, and I once again found myself slipping into the pleasantness of his visage...until disdain flooded his expression.

"You have permission?" Doubt laced his every word.

I averted my gaze and started looking at the ground for a rock. Surely, the spring thaw would be kind enough to grace me with one. It didn't need to be large. Just big enough to knock some sense into the nit.

As I searched, I answered him.

"Yes, I live here. I'm Eloise Cartwright."

"Ah. I see."

The flat tone devoid of any emotion demanded my attention. Lacking a rock, I decided to show this bore his place using the sharp edge of my tongue.

"You probably couldn't see something if it were on the tip of your nose," I said. "Now, who are you?"

"That's none of your concern."

I snorted.

"As I would expect a person guilty of trespassing to say. Go away, fiend. Leave the king's land while you still stand."

He barked out a laugh.

"Are you always this abrasive?" he asked.

"When covered in mud and dealing with an overbearing—"

"Do not call me an ass again."

"Wouldn't think of it. Pig."

His expression darkened.

"That's not to your liking, either? As you've given me no other name to call you by, Officious Grunting Pig it shall be." I smirked.

"You have a viper's tongue."

"And you have the slow wit of a cod fish. Lacking any decency, you've proven yourself to be beneath me."

"Beneath you?"

"Please do try to keep up with this conversation. Or must I speak slower?"

Pink invaded his cheeks, and I knew I'd won this battle.

"You are most fortunate I'm a decent man, or I would see you beaten."

I snorted.

"Any decent person would introduce himself. You started this by yelling in my face and tossing accusations about."

His nostrils flared in his anger, but then, to my surprise, he bowed low.

"The name's Kaven," he said.

I barely heard. My gaze was fixated on the crest adorning his cap. It was the same crest that the delivery boy had worn. All righteous pride at besting this man fled, replaced by the cold, convicted anger filling my chest.

"What is that?" I demanded.

He straightened to give me a quizzical look.

"The crest on your hat. What does it mean? Who is it for?"

The suspicion returned to his gaze.

"It's the king's crest. How can you claim to live on these lands and not know the king's crest?"

I didn't answer. My mind was racing. What did it mean that a king's messenger delivered the necklace that killed my mother? It made no sense. We were on the king's land by his decree. Why would the king favor us with land then kill one of us?

Kaven, reached out, gripping my arms.

"Answer me, woman."

That snapped me from my thoughts.

"I know nothing of the king's crest because my mother forbade us from walking the woods when the king was in residence. Now, unhand me."

His eyes narrowed.

"I don't believe you."

"I don't care what you believe. You truly are a beast. How many more of you are there at the lodge?" I asked.

His grip tightened.

"Why do you want to know?"

"So I know how many people the king has brought to push me into the mud and torment me," I lied, trying to pull myself free from his steel grasp.

He didn't budge.

I stomped on the arch of his foot.

"Release me," I demanded.

He did so immediately and scowled at me.

"Go home, Eloise Cartwright. Listen to your mother's wise words."

I hated him. I hated all who'd come with him. And I vowed to find the necklace, the boy who delivered it, and the person responsible for it all. Even if that person was the king himself.

"Do not speak of my mother. She died the day after you arrived," I said glaring.

His anger vanished from his face. Nothing replaced it. No sympathy or pity.

"How?" he asked.

I swallowed hard. I couldn't tell what I knew. Not with

him wearing the king's crest. No one would believe me that the king sent the magic amulet. Even speaking of the amulet would get me killed.

"My mother's health has been failing for years," I said instead.

"I'm sorry for your loss." He didn't sound sorry. He sounded distrustful. His next words confirmed it.

"Where is she buried?"

"In the clearing behind our home. She liked the trees and sunlight on her face."

Something shifted in his eyes, but I couldn't tell what.

"Tell me, Kaven. For how long must I avoid the woods I've called home?"

"I do not know."

He turned and left me standing in the woods, mud drying to my skirts. The birds started singing after a moment, and the small animals in the underbrush chittered at me.

"Nothing good will come of this," I said, thinking of Kaven's crest. The king's crest.

Father's warning to let go of what I knew rang in my ears once more. I'd thought I could wait until Kellen and I grieved, and she chose the future she wanted before I pursued answers. However, I now understood that I couldn't. Mother deserved more. Father had already abandoned her. I would not.

The walk home was cold and wearying. Thankfully,

there were no visitors to spot my disheveled state when I slipped into the kitchen.

Judith looked up from whatever she was stirring over the fire.

"Eloise, what happened, child?"

"The spring mud tested my agile step and showed me that I was lacking. I think a washing is in order."

Her gaze swept me from head to foot.

"The mud is in your hair, too. A simple washing will not do. A full bath is needed. Sit on the stool. Anne and I will start drawing water."

The pair had the tub before the fire and half-filled before the kitchen door opened again. Kellen walked in and stopped abruptly at the sight of me.

"Sister, did the pig drag you through the mud?"

I grinned.

"Why, yes. A pig did do this. Unfortunately, not our sweet pig. However, you've just given me a brilliant idea for a name for our dear pig."

"Oh?"

"What do you think of Kaven?"

She tilted her head and gave me a quizzical look.

"I sense a story. Would you like me to help wash your hair while you tell it?"

"Please."

Judith and Anne left the kitchen to give us privacy. Kellen helped me out of my muddy things and started removing clumps of mud from my hair as I slipped into the tub of warm water and washed my arms and face.

"Who is Kaven?" she asked.

"A dolt I met in the trees behind our house. He startled me so badly I slipped and fell. Then, the boor didn't even have the manners to help me up. Instead, he began accusing me of trespassing. He was completely rude."

"Sounds like the boys in the market."

"Very much so," I agreed. Only this one had made my heart race and may have had a hand in Mother's death. I pushed that thought from my mind as Kellen answered.

"Then, of course we will name the pig after him. I've removed as much of the mud as I can. Now, you need to go under."

I looked at the murky water and sighed.

"I wish it was warmer out. Bathing at the pond would be infinitely more enjoyable."

Kellen made a sound of agreement, which stopped abruptly as I ducked under the water. Her fingers threaded in my hair, removing more mud as I held my breath. Being underwater was one of the things I liked about the pond. Nothing but fish could touch me. No sight or sound from the real world. It was an escape from troubling thoughts. One that Kellen and I enjoyed during the sweltering heat of summer.

When I reemerged, Kellen started soaping my hair.

"While you were out playing in mud, I was in the attic,"

she said. "I found something interesting in one of the trunks pushed into a dark corner."

"What's that?"

"Letters to Mother from an old friend. Do you recall Mother ever mentioning an Elspeth?"

I shook my head.

"Nor do I. Yet, from Elspeth's letters, it would seem they were close. She apologized for leaving Mother so soon after our births and asked after us by name."

Kellen seemed intrigued by the idea that Mother had a friend. I could understand why. Although no one had said so, we'd grown up under the impression that Mother had no family. To discover Mother had an estranged cousin and, now, a friend from before our births felt odd. Why would Mother hide letters from us?

"How many letters are there?" I asked.

"A small trunk full."

"It would seem you found your hobby," I said, knowing the mystery of who Elspeth was would keep Kellen occupied for a time.

Kellen left me to sit impatiently on my own as I dried before the fire. With nothing to do but run my fingers through my hair, I dwelled on my meeting with Kaven.

I wished I hadn't met him as I had. That he hadn't been wearing that cap and crest. But that wish was purely selfish from the treacherous organ buried in my chest. My mind knew better. It was too coincidental that Mother died the day after Kaven had arrived and that he wore the king's emblem, the same as the boy who'd delivered the amulet. I needed to find the connection between Kaven and the boy; and the best way to do that was to go to the king's hunting retreat. What excuse could I give for my presence, though?

I thought of the pig and smiled. Tomorrow, the pig and I would go for a walk.

LOOKING TIRED, Maeve entered the dining room and joined us at the table. It felt odd taking meals there, but given the possibility of unexpected visitors, we had decided to follow formality for a while.

"How did everything go today?" Kellen asked Maeve as Judith served us bowls of stew.

"Well enough. We had twelve callers. Those whom Anne had pointed out as the most vapid gossips were first. The questions they asked about Margaret's passing and her place at this estate bordered on unacceptable. They weren't even trying to hide where their interests lay. Unfortunately for them, the only juicy bit they received was the lemon tartlets. I anticipate we won't see many guests tomorrow because of it. How did you two occupy yourselves today?"

"I organized the attic," Kellen said. "There is more room now if any of your possessions do not fit in Mother's room."

"Thank you for your consideration." Maeve smiled warmly at Kellen before looking at me. "What about you, Eloise? Did you find a way to keep busy today?"

"I went for a walk and fell in some mud."

"A king's servant startled her," Kellen added.

I smiled at my sister. She hated when I said anything that made me sound clumsy or incompetent in any way.

"A king's servant?" Maeve asked. "Out here?"

"This estate sits on the king's land," Kellen said. "The Royal Retreat is further along the road through the trees. Several days before you arrived, we heard dogs and learned that the king would be in residence soon."

Maeve frowned.

"That doesn't bode well for us."

"What do you mean?" I asked, trying to suppress my excitement that I might have an ally in my suspicions against the Crown.

"If the king will be in residence, it gives the gossips more reason to return during the mourning period. They will use the excuse of condolences to try to gain information about the king." She looked at me. "The fact that you're walking in the woods and running into servants is troubling, too. I wouldn't dare suggest you refrain from your walks. I believe the fresh air is good for you. However, we will need to see both of you appropriately attired in mourning gowns. We don't want to start tongues wagging. We shall go tomorrow. Judith and Anne can turn away any visitors on our behalves."

The idea of going to town did not appeal to me. The trip would mean a regrettable delay in my walk to the king's estate. Based on the look on Kellen's face, she was likewise put out by the news. Though, the likely reason for that was due to the band of bullies who'd enjoyed tormenting us.

Maeve didn't seem to notice either of our subdued agreements.

"Judith mentioned that you lost a necklace because of vermin. Perhaps while we are in town, we should look for a house cat as well," she said.

CHAPTER SIX

"SOME AIRING WILL REMOVE THE MUSTY SMELL IN NO TIME," Maeve said, holding a handkerchief to her nose.

I nodded and glanced at Kellen, who sat beside me in our small, seldom used family carriage. She watched out the window as I'd been doing. However, one wouldn't be able to tell if it was due to the need for fresh air or her interest in the passing countryside. At times, I envied her composure. At other times, I worried for her. She kept so much inside.

Reaching over, I clasped her hand. Her fingers curled around mine, the only acknowledgement she gave the gesture. That she continued to hold my hand was enough to know what she was truly feeling. My other hand clenched into a fist, and I almost hoped that the boys would be at the market again. My anger from my encounter with Kaven remained intact, and if I couldn't use him as a target, I'd find a substitute. There was no shortage of boorish swine in Towdown.

"I'm at a disadvantage," Maeve said interrupting my thoughts. "I'm unsure which shops are suitable for producing quality mourning attire."

"We usually see Madame Thread," Kellen said. "She's affordable and adequate."

Maeve blinked at her.

"Adequate is hardly an endorsement. I shouldn't imagine she's very respected with a name like Madame Thread."

I coughed lightly in the handkerchief I held in my free hand. However, my attempt to hide my humor wasn't lost on Maeve.

"I sound pretentious, don't I?" she said ruefully. "I don't mean to be. I only understand the importance of presentation. While you both are lovely, those who've visited us would still judge the cut and quality of the cloth covering you and try to find ways in which it is lacking. Unfortunately, with the King soon to be in residence, I fear we are not yet free of unwanted attention. To protect both of you from the ridicule of wagging tongues, I would like to see you attired by a seamstress of note."

"We understand," I said. Maeve's concern for us was touching. And, I appreciated that she wasn't attempting to shelter us from our harsh reality.

"Madame Todd's is well known and frequented by

many of the gentry," Kellen said. "However, I'm not sure we brought enough coin for that."

Maeve waved away Kellen's concern.

"Your father's arrangement with me means you have no need to concern yourself with expenses."

Kellen smiled in acceptance, a mask to hide what she truly felt, and I struggled to do the same. What had Father been thinking to not only put the burden of two grieving girls on Maeve but also to expect her to cover our expenses while he was gone?

The carriage rolled through town, the wheels grating against the cobblestone that lined the streets of the more affluent districts. I watched the people, and a thought wormed its way into my mind. Would my family still be whole if we'd lived in town like everyone else?

Kellen's hold in my hand loosened, and I realized the carriage was slowing. I looked out at Madame Todd's and saw the swathes of prettily colored fabrics in the window.

"What if she doesn't make mourning garb?" I asked.

Maeve smiled at me. "No one refuses Lady Grimmoire, my darling."

The door opened, and Hugh offered his hand to Maeve. She nodded regally to him then stepped to the ground to wait for us, so we could enter the store together.

A floral scent, much like spring's first blooms, wrapped around us. It was a scent I rather enjoyed.

One of the girls welcomed us and asked how she could be of assistance.

"We're in need of two mourning wardrobes. At least three gowns each. Two suitable for daily wear, which includes accepting visitors. One for larger gatherings."

The girl hesitated.

"Will this be a problem?" Maeve asked.

"Not at all. May I have your names, please?"

"I am Lady Grimmoire, guardian to Eloise and Kellen Cartwright." She gestured to me then Kellen as she made the introductions.

"If you would care to have a seat, you may browse the sketches while I ask Madame Todd to join us."

Maeve smiled as the girl hurried off, leaving us to find our own way to the chairs placed at the left of the door.

"And that is how it is done," she said softly. "Note that there is no black fabric on display. Customers don't want to be reminded of mourning when shopping for pretty things. I'm also certain they do not keep enough fabric on hand for six gowns."

"Three each does seem a bit much," Kellen said.

"I promise I am not leading you astray from our goals," Maeve said. "Presentation and respecting your mother's memory are foremost."

She picked up a sketchbook and handed it to us.

"Look through this and find two gown styles you find suitable. I'll pick the third."

"Are we really going to a larger gathering while in mourning?" I asked.

"I'm not yet certain. However, it is prudent to be prepared."

Kellen and I looked through the book. There weren't many options that were as plain as we were used to. We selected our two dress styles and had just handed the book to Maeve when the girl returned with an older woman.

"Welcome to my shop. Paulette has told me you would like six mourning gowns. Have you any particular styles in mind?"

Maeve encouraged Kellen and me to show the gowns we'd selected, then she took the book and opened to the last page. The dress there had a full, flowing skirt that belled out in an elegant display with lace embellishments. The heartline bodice and trim sleeves looked exquisite and far too formal for anything we could possibly attend while in mourning.

Kellen and I shared a look.

"Are you certain you want this in black and not a soft grey?" the Madame asked.

"Yes, black. My wards are determined to be in mourning for the three months they are allowed. Their dear mother made them swear not to mourn a day beyond that. She was such a selfless woman, our Margaret. She knows these dears are of an age to marry and didn't want her passing to prevent her children from finding their happiness."

Madame Todd smiled and gave us an affectionate look.

"You are both lovely. I can see why your mother made

you vow not to grieve too long. Black it is, then." She looked at Maeve. "How soon would you like these completed?"

"The first gown is needed tomorrow. All of the gowns within seven days. You will be appropriately compensated for the rush and awarded more if you can have them done sooner."

Madame bowed her head in a gracious acknowledgement.

"Come. Let us start with the measurements."

While Madame spoke in quiet tones with Maeve, two of the seamstresses led Kellen and me to the back of the shop where we stripped down to our underthings and were thoroughly measured.

When we finished, Maeve was waiting alone near the front of the store.

"Just a few more stops, my darlings," she said as we left Madame Todd's.

Hugh helped us into the carriage and closed the door. The conveyance bounced as he settled his weight into the driver's seat. A moment later, he called to the horses, and we started forward.

"Why do we need a dress tomorrow?" Kellen asked.

"And why did you say we'd promised not to mourn more than three months?" I added.

"The answer to both questions is simple. Presentation and appearance. The gossips will now know there is a timeframe for your grieving and will not judge you harshly if there is a slip because it's your mother's wish that you not grieve too long. The supposed vow paints your mother in a very gracious and irreproachable light. The request for an immediate gown shows just how deeply you're both grieving."

"While I understand the reasons for it, I disagree with lying," Kellen said.

Maeve quietly considered us before speaking.

"Although your mother did not ask you to make such a vow, do you think she would have if she'd known her time was near?"

"Yes," I said. "She wouldn't want us to grieve long."

The carriage started to slow. When I glanced out the window, I saw we were off the cobbled path on a dirt side street.

"I would like you both to wait here," Maeve said. "This shop is not suitable for unwed girls."

"What is it?" I asked.

"An herbalist. I find I need tinctures during my monthly cycle to help control the pain and bleeding. Did your mother speak to you of such things?"

Kellen and I both shook our heads.

"Should your monthly cycles ever cause you issue, please do feel you can come speak to me. I wouldn't want either of you to suffer when there are remedies."

The carriage stopped, and the door opened. In the silence that followed Maeve's departure, Kellen reached for my hand.

"I am not speaking to her about my monthly cycles."

I giggled.

Kellen and I started bleeding the same time years ago. Our cycles had never caused us much pain. Other than having to deal with extra clothing, it wasn't something I'd given much thought. But Kellen was right. Speaking with Maeve about monthly cycles wasn't something I was about to do, either.

It didn't take long for Maeve to return to us.

"Next stop is the cobbler."

"I would prefer to return home," Kellen said.

Maeve frowned.

"Are you feeling unwell?"

I knew that Kellen was feeling fine. However, the best cobbler, which is where Maeve would probably insist we go, was near the market district.

"Kellen is fine," I said, giving my sister's hand a reassuring squeeze. "It's only that our shoes are still in very good condition. It's unnecessary to purchase another pair."

Maeve smiled.

"Presentation and appearance, my darlings. Now, who is the best cobbler?"

Kellen answered, her voice carefully neutral.

When the carriage stopped, she and I both glanced out the windows while Maeve waited for the door. Kellen's fingers twitched in mine, and I followed her gaze. The boys who'd tormented us during our last excursion were leaning against a building not far away. All eyes were on our carriage. As soon as we stepped down, they would see us.

I couldn't stop the slow grin that parted my lips.

"Please don't cause trouble," Kellen said as Maeve stepped out.

"I won't start it," I said, moving to the door.

"I wasn't talking to you," she answered, making my grin widen.

"No smiling, Eloise," Maeve said softly. "Please appear suitably aggrieved."

My humor immediately fled. She was right. Now wasn't the time, no matter how badly I wished to strike out, to relieve myself of this impotent anger festering inside of me.

Maeve opened the shop door for us and let me step inside first. The cobbler immediately looked up from his work.

"Eloise Cartwright," he said. His brow lifted in surprise. "Kellen too. I didn't expect to see you so soon. Is there a problem with the fit of your boots?"

"No, sir," I answered. "We're here for a new pair."

Maeve stepped forward.

"My girls need something more refined to go with their mourning gowns."

"I see. You've come to the right place, miss..."

"Lady Grimmoire," Maeve said with a small smile. "How long will it take to complete a new pair?"

"I have a few orders to finish but could have them ready by the end of the week."

"That would be lovely. Do you need measurements?"

He shook his head.

"I took them a few weeks back."

"Splendid. Would you have time to look at my shoes? I'm afraid the heel has come loose."

"Of course."

"Girls, if you would like to look around the market for a set of black ribbons, we can leave as soon as we're done."

Kellen nodded and started toward the door before I could come up with a suitable excuse for us to remain with Maeve. Outside, the light blinded me for a moment.

"Where are you two off to?" Hugh asked from the top of the carriage.

"Hair ribbons," Kellen said.

"Try to stay out of trouble." The slight shake of his head that accompanied his words said just how much he believed we could.

Side by side, we walked away from the cobbler and headed toward the busy market. The boys watched us pass, their expressions laced with boredom.

"Is there any chance that they will ignore us?" Kellen asked.

"Doubtful."

"Fighting with them will reflect poorly on Mother's memory."

"I'm sure Mother would understand."

Kellen agreed.

I knew the exact moment the boys left their position

against the building and started following us. A tingle ran down my back like a sixth sense. They drew closer but did nothing more than follow us.

Pretending not to notice them, Kellen and I stopped at a booth that displayed pretty ribbons.

"Do you have any in black?" Kellen asked.

"We do, miss." The woman turned her back to us and looked through a small chest she had on another table.

"Didn't expect to see you two so soon," a familiar voice said from behind us.

"We had rather hoped to never see you again," I said, without turning.

The woman searching through the ribbons glanced our way. I gave her a small smile.

"How many ribbons are you looking for?" she asked.

"Four please," Kellen said.

The woman handed us our ribbons, and Kellen gave her a copper. When we turned, the boys were no longer behind us but, instead, were looking at another stall's wares a fair distance away. They were obviously in a mood to torment us. A pot to the head apparently hadn't made them any smarter.

"Hugh would probably like a biscuit," Kellen said softly.

I smiled at my sister's cunning. The stall that sold the best biscuits belonged to a nice, old man tending a booth off the beaten track, away from prying eyes that might witness any scuffle between two mourning girls and a bunch of bullying boys.

"Hugh rarely gets a biscuit. You're very kind to think of him," I said.

We continued down the main thoroughfare, past our group of tormentors. It didn't take long for the boys to start following us again. Kellen and I wove our way through the crowds around the vendor stalls and took a left down one of the side streets.

The scent of butter and baking bread tickled my nose. The best biscuit vendor didn't charge much, which enabled everyone to enjoy his creations. Unfortunately, catering to the lesser folk meant others refused to patronize him.

When the man saw us approaching, he smiled and readied six biscuits. Enough for everyone in our household. He knew us well.

"Good morning, Ladies," he said, already holding up the bundle.

"Good morning." Kellen handed over the necessary coin with, perhaps, a little extra.

A scrape of noise from the alley's entrance briefly drew the man's gaze, and I knew a conflict would be unavoidable before returning to Maeve. Kellen understood the same.

"Would you happen to have any day-old biscuits?" she asked. "I do enjoy feeding the songbirds."

"My biscuits never last that long," he said. "However, I do have a few that are too hard to sell. My grandson is trying to help with the baking, but he doesn't have the eye yet to know when to remove them from the oven." He showed us a dozen dark brown biscuits.

"We'll take all of them," Kellen said.

The baker handed over the bundle, which I accepted while Kellen gave another coin.

"Thank you!" I called as we moved away.

Happy that we'd helped the baker as much as he'd helped us, Kellen and I moved down the alley at a brisk pace, not toward the main thoroughfare but deeper into the quiet areas that would bring us back around to the cobbler.

I knew the boys were following and hoped the baker wouldn't pay them any attention. It didn't take long after we rounded a corner for the boys to start heckling.

"Which do you think will speak to us today?" Alfie asked.

"It will be Cinder for certain," Carver answered. "Snow never speaks. Frozen lips, that one."

"At least for us."

"Maybe today that will change. What do you say, Snow? How about we try a kiss to thaw that heart of ice?"

Laughter echoed behind us, and I untied my bag of biscuits.

"The birds would have liked them," Kellen said.

"I'll save what I can," I said.

Gripping a biscuit, I turned and threw in one fluid motion, immediately reaching for another.

The first brown projectile hit Carver square between

the eyes and exploded in a cloud of caramel colored crumbs. He cried out and clutched his forehead.

The second biscuit was already flying through the air and hit Alfie in the temple because he had turned to look at Carver. Alfie grunted and clutched his head.

Grinning, I looked at Samuel. He knew what was happening and batted away the biscuit I'd aimed at his head before it could connect.

"I didn't think you were stupid enough to try taunting us again after the pot," I said. "But, perhaps it only addled your wits enough to think you can win this."

A slow grin spread on Carver's face, and a tingle of awareness alerted me that we were no longer alone.

I pivoted on my heel and saw Maeve striding toward us. Her gaze swept over Kellen and me before focusing on the boys.

"What is the meaning of this?" she demanded.

All three boys shrugged, their expressions innocent.

"We don't know why they started throwing biscuits at us," Alfie said.

"Neither one is stable," Carver said.

"Mental, they are," Samuel added.

"I know very well they are quite stable despite the recent passing of their mother," Maeve said. "I'm curious why you thought to torment two grieving girls. Perhaps you are the ones without wit, and it would be best that I do speak with your parents. I would like your names, please."

Panicked expressions blossomed on their faces before they turned heel and ran.

Maeve looked at both of us.

"Are you two all right?" she asked.

I felt a little guilty that she was concerned about us when we were the ones who had enabled this trouble.

"Yes," Kellen said. "We're well. Those boys said nothing they haven't said before."

"You think they would be smarter and stay away, given your sister's accurate aim," Maeve said with a small smile at me.

I grinned in return.

"Now, I think it's about time we did something so these boys no longer bother you. Do you know their names?"

Kellen and I both gave hesitant nods.

"If you would be kind enough to direct me to the first home, I will indeed speak with their parents."

At each home, we stood behind Maeve as she recapped what she had seen and explained how the boys had been following us during multiple visits to town. When she suggested that the boys were teasing us because "the dear lads" didn't know the proper way to court a young woman who held their interests, I wanted to hide in my room for a good year. That she then offered to teach the boys the proper practice of courtship and suggested that the boys could renew their attempts at courting once they understood the rules only made my mortification worse. Thankfully, she reiterated such a courtship could not be before our mourning periods were up.

We left stunned parents in our wake. I heard one woman say to her husband that he better get the lash out and find their boy. If I hadn't been so horrified about the talk of courting, I would have laughed.

Back in the carriage, Kellen and I quietly stared at Maeve.

"You don't really want them to court us, do you?" I asked.

Maeve laughed.

"As a well-dressed woman of means, if I'd gone into those homes accusing the boys of bad behavior, I doubt they would have been punished. There's a line between those with wealth and those without. However, because I went in there as a woman of means and treated those parents as if we were equal, they listened. They will see a ruined chance at a good match—because distaste was clearly on your faces—and those boys will not be able to sit without pain for a week."

I leaned back into my seat, grinning.

"That is truly brilliant."

"Thank you," she said.

It was good to know that Kellen and I would be able to return to town for the dresses without needing to worry about the usual harassment. If only Maeve could so easily deal with the other issues in my life. That thought robbed me of any remaining humor, and I looked out the window.

I desperately wanted to confide in her. She'd handled the situation with our tormentors with a cleverness I admired. But more importantly, she hadn't thought for a moment that Kellen and I were the problem. Yet, it was that strength of conviction that stayed my tongue. Would she be a strong ally and as passionate as I was about uncovering Mother's murderer? Or would she be like my father and ardently insist on my silence?

Unable to risk the latter, I made up my mind. I alone would continue to bear the burden of knowledge that someone had had a hand in Mother's death. And, I alone would risk myself to expose that person.

Tonight, I would go to the king's estate. My mother's murderer would be named before I slept.

CHAPTER SEVEN

"THANK YOU FOR ANOTHER LOVELY MEAL," I SAID TO JUDITH as she took my plate.

I nudged Kellen under the table with my foot. As usual, she didn't acknowledge it.

"I think I'll go for a walk," I said standing.

Maeve frowned and glanced at the fading light through the window.

"Are you certain you want to walk now? It will be dark soon."

"It's the best time of day to walk. I'll be fine."

"Perhaps you should take Hugh with you," she suggested as Judith picked up Kellen's plate.

I didn't miss the poke that Kellen gave Judith and suppressed my grin.

"There's no need to worry, Maeve," Judith said. "Eloise

has walked these woods in the dark plenty of times. There's nothing for her to fear."

"Go on then," Maeve said kindly, "and enjoy your walk. Don't stay out too long, though, or I will worry."

It felt odd hearing those words. My mother hadn't ever worried about my excursions.

Giving Maeve a small smile to show I appreciated her concern, I followed Judith from the room.

"What are you two up to now?" Judith asked when the door closed behind us.

"Up to? I only wanted a walk alone and, given the time of day and Maeve's good sense about appearances, didn't think she'd approve."

Judith snorted as I grabbed my cloak.

"So you thought to pull me in?"

"You're a solid voice of reason, Judith. That's why we always pull you in." I grinned and waved goodbye before letting myself out.

The cool night air wrapped around me as my humor faded. I set out for the king's estate, forgoing the pig and using the path to Mother's grave. The moon's full light guided me easily to the mound of dirt and the small pear tree that was thriving. I paused for a moment to speak to Mother.

"Lady Grimmoire was a sight to see, today," I said softly. "It's nice to have someone champion us. But it should be Father here. I try not to be angry with him. You know I do. But how can I not?"

The wind shook the sapling, and I noted the tiny branches protruding from its wisp-thin trunk. "Don't worry about Kellen or me. We're fine. And I'll keep my promises. I love you."

With that, I continued on my way, following the same route as before. I knew most of these woods as well as I knew the corners of my own home.

Weaving through the trees, I slowly made my way toward the king's estate. The low murmur of voices, the soft baying of dogs, and the occasional snort from a horse reached my ears before I saw the torch lights through the branches.

I stepped behind a thick tree trunk and pulled the dark hood over my head before peeking out to watch the people move about. Many of them wore caps with the king's crest. None looked as small as the boy who'd delivered the necklace, however. That didn't mean he wasn't here, only that I needed patience or perhaps courage to steal into their ranks.

The men moving about the yard were taking pieces of furniture and trunks off the back of several wagons and carrying them into the large retreat.

Kellen and I had always wanted to explore inside but had never been brave enough to break a lock. I couldn't say if it had been due to fear of the Crown's wrath or Mother's.

Amidst all of the workers, I spotted Kaven. The cap was missing from his head this time. So was his jacket. My stomach tightened at the sight of the light cloth straining against his arms as he carried an oilcloth covered painting toward the retreat. He really needed a better tailor...the ass.

"What are we looking at?" Kellen asked suddenly.

I jumped and turned to smack her arm. She grinned at me.

"Pull up your hood and stand behind a tree. We're going to get caught if you're not careful," I said softly.

She moved to the other side of me, still smiling.

"Quite the din they are making. Not conducive for the mending of a broken heart. What do you see when you stare out there?" she asked.

Kellen's appearance changed my plans for the evening. I couldn't very well lurk closer and search for the boy without her demanding to know why. So, I moved away from the tree and tugged her arm to indicate I was ready to leave.

"Nothing that interests me."

We didn't speak again until we put considerable distance between us and the retreat.

"Why did you follow me?" I asked.

"I was curious what warranted a kick to my shin at dinner."

"The scare you gave me while feeding the pig warranted the shin."

She chuckled.

"When I ran into Kaven, he was hedgy about how many men were with him. I want to know why."

"And did you learn why?"

I shook my head.

"Perhaps it's just me, but something feels wrong about the king's sudden use of the retreat. Why now?"

"You mean, why right when Mother dies?" Kellen added softly.

"Yes."

She exhaled slowly.

"You're angry, Eloise, and you want someone to blame. Please believe that I understand. But, finding blame will not change what's done." She reached out and took my hand in hers, stopping our progress.

"Don't let your anger goad you into something you will regret. I can't lose you, too."

I wrapped my arms around her and hugged her fiercely.

"Never, Kellen. You will never lose me. I swear I will never act so rashly as to cause you pain."

She hugged me in return.

"I believe you."

I TURNED this way and that before the mirror. Black wasn't my color. My golden hair and naturally sun-kissed skin robbed the look of its intended severity.

"You look lovely, miss," one of the girls kneeling at my feet said.

"Thank you," I replied automatically. I didn't care how I

looked. I hated the dress and what it meant. But, I would endure.

Beside me, Kellen scarcely moved as her skirt was likewise hemmed. Unlike me, the dark color suited her. Pale and regally elegant, my sister would cause many a head to turn while wearing that dress. Not something she would enjoy. Thankfully, our time in these frocks would be short, and there would be more to our day than fittings.

As Maeve had predicted, the arrival of condoling visitors wasn't yet finished. So, she'd sent us to town to fetch our mourning garb without her. Neither Kellen nor I minded the chance to escape. In fact, I was quite looking forward to a stroll through the market.

"We're finished, miss. Would you like us to wrap your other dress?"

"Please," Kellen said, answering for me.

I realized, then, that our walk through the market would be done in our mourning dresses. It killed some of my anticipation.

I glanced at Kellen in the mirror and met her gaze. I knew she understood and felt the same.

When we left the shop, we returned to the wagon with our dresses.

"Where did Judith go?" I asked Hugh, who was charged with watching over any purchases Judith brought to the wagon.

"There's some cook she knows in one of them fancy

houses. She went to ask for a pastry recipe to impress Lady Grimmoire."

"We're going to walk to the market," Kellen said.

He nodded and remained quiet as we left him.

One of the best things about Hugh was that he didn't judge us or try to dissuade us from our actions. When I'd asked him why, he told me that was what parents were for. After that, Kellen and I started bringing Hugh treats. He knew a bribe when he saw one and happily ate what we brought and kept quiet about any antics he might overhear or see.

Kellen and I had barely reached the edge of the market when we spotted Carver. He stood in his usual place. As I watched, a woman walked past, and the boy bowed formally. When he straightened, I saw his bruised cheek. He looked across the way at an older man who sat on a short stool. The man's scowl never left his face as he nodded at the boy.

I thought of Maeve's explanation the day before and guilt slowed my steps.

"He was not beaten because of us but because of his own actions. The bruise is his consequence, not yours," Kellen said.

She looped her arm through mine and propelled me forward. When we came abreast with our tormentor, she stopped and faced him.

He bowed low.

"Miss Kellen. Miss Eloise. Please forgive my coarse

behavior these past months. I hope when I come to call, you will be able to look at me with favor."

"Do not come to call, and I will find much favor in your lack of presence," Kellen said.

If it was possible, the boy's expression deadened further; and I felt a wealth of pity for him despite Kellen's warning not to.

"You can call on me," I said. "Do not expect to find favor after only one courtly bow and a few kind words, though. The deeds define the man, not the pretty words that fall from his lips."

Nudging Kellen, I started us on our way again.

"You were too kind to him."

"Perhaps kindness is what he needed. In all the trouble we have caused, never once did Mother or Father raise a hand to us. How differently would we have behaved if they had?" I asked then shrugged. "Does violence beget violence? If so, does kindness then beget kindness? I believe Mother thought so."

Kellen was quiet for several long moments.

"You're very like her," she said finally.

"How so? I've never seen Mother throw biscuits at anyone."

A smile briefly tugged Kellen's lips.

"Your temper might get the best of you, but you do think of others and how they feel. Mother did that."

"You do, too."

She didn't answer.

After doing a loop of the market, we returned to the wagon and found Judith waiting with Hugh.

"We're sorry we took so long," Kellen said.

"Nonsense," Judith said. "It's good for both of you to be seen. Maeve will be pleased you walked the market with your new dresses."

I looked down at my skirt and realized I'd forgotten what I wore. How would I ever survive three months of nothing but black? The constant reminder of what was now missing in my life would eat holes through me.

"We're ready to leave if you are," Kellen said, releasing me so she could climb aboard the wagon.

I joined her, more than ready to return home so I could escape into the woods once more. Side by side, we silently endured the jostling return to the estate. Kellen excused herself to further organize the attic, which I knew meant she was still reading Mother's letters.

"I think I'll go for a walk and visit Mother," I said.

Judith absently nodded and went inside.

My feet carried me down the familiar path through the trees, and I stopped at the sight of Mother's grave. The sapling, which had been the length of my forearm when I planted it, now stretched to the height of my hips. No longer was it a single shoot but an actual small tree with several branches that jutted several inches from the thin trunk.

I moved closer, knowing there was only one explanation for the tree's rapid growth. Yet, there was no tingle or unnatural spark when I gently touched a branch. Staring at the tree, I hoped it wasn't born from the unnatural magic that had claimed my mother's life but rather from the love that had once nurtured us.

"Be at peace, Mother. Know that we are well and continue to love you, too," I said softly before continuing on.

Unlike the prior evening, the king's estate lay quiet. There was no wagon in the yard or restless horses. The lack of movement and noise made the entire thing feel sinister.

I debated sneaking inside but didn't trust the unexpected silence. Rubbing my arms, I leaned against the tree and huddled further into the warmth of my cloak. I stayed like that until my fingers and nose grew cold then gave up and started home.

It wasn't the building that interested me but the people within. There was no point lingering if there were no people to observe. My thoughts went to Kaven instead of the delivery boy, and I hurried away.

CREEPING DOWN THE STAIRS, I listened to the soft murmur of voices as I carefully edged my way along the wall. Kellen wasn't even out of bed yet. I couldn't imagine Maeve was too pleased with whomever thought to call at this hour.

Successfully reaching the dining room without

detection, I slipped inside and went to the kitchen. The warmth of the room enveloped me.

"It's a bit early for a visitor, isn't it?" I asked, looking for my breakfast.

Anne moved about the kitchen in a bit of a frenzy.

"It is. Judith and I aren't yet ready."

"Can I help?"

"Please."

She set me to work while she started something for breakfast. I didn't mind rolling out pastry dough and cutting the required shapes under Anne's instruction, but it wasn't something Judith typically entrusted to anyone.

"Where is Judith?" I asked after I stacked the first set of thin dough disks. Layered with berries, it looked like it would become a delicate, towering treat once baked.

"I'm not sure. She wasn't here when I woke. I think she might have gone to town again to check with the cook about this recipe. There's nothing noted to sweeten it. I know Judith wanted it to be just right to impress Maeve, but I can't wait. We need something to serve the guests."

"What if we sprinkle a bit of sugar on the top?" I asked. "I've seen Judith glaze dough with the whites of an egg to get mint leaves to stick. We could do that to get the sugar to stick."

Anne paused her sorting of berries to consider it.

"We'll do half that way," she said. "On the chance it doesn't work well."

I nodded and started glazing and sugaring. In no time,

the treats were baking in the oven, and I was at the table eating my egg.

Kellen strolled into the kitchen just after I cracked my shell. She had dark circles under her eyes and yawned as she walked.

"It's a bit early for visitors, isn't it?" she said, echoing my earlier question.

I grinned as Anne snorted.

"Sometimes, I swear the pair of you speak to each other with your minds."

"That would be a helpful trick," I said.

"Unfortunately, such a trait would likely see us sent to the forest," Kellen said, smothering another yawn. "Is there an extra egg?"

I took pity on her and fetched an egg.

"You were in bed before I was," I said. "How can you be so tired?"

Kellen shrugged and started eating. I considered her for a moment and knew I couldn't allow her to stay in the house another day. She wasn't doing well, and it had nothing to do with Mother's letters. I'd noticed it yesterday, too, in the way she'd been more subdued than usual.

"Since there's a visitor," I said. "Would you like to walk to town with me? We can visit the bookseller and find something to ease our boredom."

"That's a fair distance to walk while carrying books," she said.

"Judith likely took the wagon. We can meet her and gain a ride home."

"Then, a visit to the bookseller sounds like the thing." Kellen took a bite of her egg and nodded as if agreeing with herself.

As soon as we finished and helped Anne take the pretty pastries out of the oven, we left. The sun was out and the breeze absent for a nice change. I breathed deeply and tipped my head back.

"This is perfect."

"It is," Kellen agreed.

We'd barely made it past the shed when Hugh called out.

"Where are you two off to?"

"To town for books," I said.

"Do you want me to hitch the wagon?"

I stopped and frowned.

"The wagon is here?"

"Where else would it be?" he asked.

I glanced at Kellen.

"Judith wouldn't have walked to town with guests arriving at any time," she said.

"I agree. If she's not in town, then where is she?"

Kellen and I split up with Hugh. We checked the privy, the animal pens, Mother's grave, and everywhere else we could think of. Finally, we went inside to speak with Anne.

Her expression turned troubled when we related what we'd learned, and she glanced at the door.

"Should we tell Maeve?"

I understood her hesitation. Although Judith had been with us as long as Kellen and I could remember, would Maeve see Judith as hired help who abandoned her post or like a missing member of our family? Yet, with guests still arriving every day, we would be hard pressed to keep Judith's absence hidden for long.

"Maeve has followed our lead in everything to do with this household," Kellen said. "We have no reason to doubt she will continue to do so."

Anne nodded and left the room. Several minutes later, she returned with Maeve who gave us all a concerned look.

"I sent our visitor off with some pastries for her boys. Where have you all looked for Judith and where haven't we yet checked?" she asked.

We listed off where we'd already been and struggled to think of where else to look.

"While you think, I'm going to send Hugh to town with the wagon on the slim chance Judith did indeed walk. I'm sure our dear cook is well," she said, setting her hand on my arm and giving it a quick squeeze before leaving.

"What about the berry patch?" Kellen asked, pointing at the almost empty clay bowl. "Perhaps she went for more berries."

There was only one type of berry that was ripe this time of year. The tiny, dark fruits matured in the early spring within their thorny bramble. They weren't easy to find or easy to pick, but we were lucky enough to have a single patch on the king's land. It wasn't too far from the house.

"She should be back by now," I said, already moving toward the door.

The yard was quiet as Kellen and I left. My sister's steps matched mine as we hurried through the trees.

The patch came into sight along with a splash of white on the ground. I lifted my skirts and ran forward.

Judith's apron lay in the decaying mess of last year's leaves. Tiny berries rested on the material.

Lifting my gaze, I looked around the patch.

"She's gone," Kellen said flatly.

"But where?"

CHAPTER EIGHT

I BENT AND PICKED UP THE APRON, FEELING THE CHILL IN THE material.

"Anne said that Judith was gone when she woke," I said. "That meant Judith had to have come out here at first light."

Even if she had come out in the middle of the night, there wasn't anything in these woods that would bother her. Wild pigs were too hunted to be much of a nuisance. Any deer would be more likely to run than to attack. And wolves hadn't been seen in years. I'd heard rumors that after a sickness had hit Drisdall, they'd been hunted to the point that they'd all fled to the Dark Forest. Nothing here would have harmed her. Certainly nothing would have removed her apron and—

The sudden baying of hounds jerked my attention from the apron in my hands.

"Kellen, go home and tell the others what we found. I'm going to walk further and see if anyone at the king's estate has seen her."

Kellen caught my arm before I could walk off.

"Just observe from a distance," she said. "We can send Hugh to ask after her."

I nodded.

The brisk walk to the king's retreat didn't cool my temper or ease my fear. Where else could Judith have gone, if not there?

Stepping with care, I made my way to the same tree as the night before. Through the bramble and barren branches, I watched Kaven walk the well-trampled yard as he fed the hounds. He was speaking, but the hounds were making too much noise to distinguish his words.

Tree by tree, I moved closer, needing to hear. With the wind in my favor, the hounds ignored me and continued their harassment of Kaven for their meal.

"Down, you greedy mutts. There's enough for all of you. Fresh too. Just this morning."

My eyes widened, and I looked at the meat in his hand again, my stomach rolling.

He stopped throwing meat from the bucket to pat the head of one of the dogs.

"I know how you like it," he said with a chuckle. "Juicy and dripping and still warm."

I gagged.

"You best appreciate the effort I went through. This stag

wasn't easy to bring down. But, it had a rack as big as any I've seen."

I breathed out a sigh of relief and let my gaze sweep over the yard. Nothing seemed out of place from the last time I'd watched the retreat. While I still firmly placed the fault of my mother's death on the Crown, I wasn't yet certain I could place Judith's disappearance there, too.

When Kaven turned away, I left my hiding place and returned home.

Maeve was waiting by the kitchen door when I entered the yard. Her worried expression changed to one of relief when she saw me.

"Oh, Eloise. I know I have no right, but I was so worried when Kellen said what you'd found then left you in the woods alone."

She embraced me firmly, and I could feel a tremble running through her. Guilt had me hugging her in return.

"I'm sorry, Maeve. I needed to know if Judith perhaps had a run-in with the king's hounds."

She pulled back to look me in the eye.

"Please tell me you did not accuse the king of taking our housemaid."

I smiled a little, knowing such a thought probably sent her into a panic, given her stance on appearances.

"No. I swear there were no accusations. I didn't even go to the door, just watched from the trees and saw a servant feeding the hounds. They seemed tame and unlikely to attack a person."

"Good. Please don't fret over Judith. I sent Hugh to town to look for her. Perhaps the apron was forgotten from yesterday."

I nodded although I didn't agree. Judith wasn't one to forget an apron in the woods.

Maeve's expression of worry softened as she looked at me. She reached out and patted my cheek.

"I can see you don't believe that's the case. You've suffered so much already. I would spare you any further troubling news if I could."

I believed her and wished again that I could confide in her. That I wouldn't need to carry the weight of my suspicions on my own.

"What is it?" she said with a small frown. "Your expression changed just now."

"It's nothing," I said, easing toward the kitchen door. She didn't stop me.

Inside, Anne was busy cutting more disks.

"Can I help?" I asked as I took of my cloak and hung it on a peg.

"Thank you, but no. This task is to keep me from worrying," Anne said.

"Where's Kellen?"

"Resting," Maeve said as she came in the door behind me. "I insisted. She looked as if she'd barely slept last night."

I nodded and with nothing else to do, drifted from the kitchen and found myself standing in the sitting room near the lounge that Mother favored.

"Was that her spot?" Maeve asked softly behind me.

"Yes. She loved the sun on her face and watching the wind in the trees."

Maeve moved to stand beside me, and together we stared out the window for several long moments.

"I know I am not your mother. Or your sister. And that you have no reason to confide in me. But I am here to listen if you have a need."

The offer proved too much of a temptation when I needed it most.

"The day my mother died, we heard hounds in the woods. Thinking it might be poachers, Hugh went to warn them off of the king's land. He returned to say it wasn't poachers, but the king's contingent here to prepare the retreat for the arrival of the king."

I turned from the window and sat in the chair I favored. The one that faced Mother's lounge. Maeve sat beside me in Kellen's usual chair. She didn't speak, just waited for me to continue.

"It wasn't long after that a messenger boy appeared with a wrapped box. We thought it a gift from Father. However, the necklace inside wasn't a gift, and it wasn't from father. The moment the pendant touched Mother's skin, an unnatural light lit her eyes, and she died."

Maeve's expression filled with shock and sorrow. I continued before she could interrupt.

"When I ran into the king's servant, he was wearing the

same insignia on his cap as the messenger who'd delivered the necklace. It's the king's insignia." I gripped my hands in my lap, trying not to blurt out the blatant accusation that waited on the tip of my tongue. "I don't believe we will find Judith anywhere in town."

"I see," Maeve said. She looked out the window for a moment before clasping my hand.

"While the evidence surely leads one to believe there is only one conclusion, I cannot help but wonder what purpose the Crown would have for killing your mother. It makes no sense. There is no benefit. I am not disagreeing with you, dear one. I'm only stating that you need to consider carefully what would motivate the single most important person in this kingdom to care enough about your mother to kill her."

"I don't know." I sighed and studied the light pattern on Mother's lounge. Maeve patted my hands and left me to my thoughts.

She was right. There was no logical motivation for the king to concern himself over Mother's fate. Yet, we lived in a home on the king's land for a reason. Why?

I wasn't sure how long I sat there before I heard the faint rumble of a wagon in the yard. Hurrying through the house, I went to the kitchen, the first place Hugh would go if it were him and the last place a guest would go if we were so unfortunate.

The door opened, and Anne stopped her pastry cutting to look up at Hugh.

None of his usual humor lit his eyes. In fact, they looked quite dull.

"There wasn't any sign of her. I asked at all the usual haunts." He paused for a moment then turned around and left without another word.

Anne and I shared a look. Neither of us spoke. She picked up her knife and went back to cutting her pastries.

Angry at fate, I departed the kitchen and found my way upstairs. Kellen was sleeping soundly on top of her covers. The dark circles, that were under her eyes earlier, were missing. Taking care not to wake her, I joined her on the bed. It wasn't something I'd done in a long time. But I needed the comfort of my twin.

The gentle touch of a finger on my eyelid woke me some time later.

I opened my eyes and stared at Kellen.

"You snore," she said softly. "It scared the mice away."

"I do not snore. You do," I said, repeating the same thing we always said to each other when she found me in her bed.

She studied me for a moment.

"Something has been troubling you for a long time. Why haven't you confided in me?"

"Because you're hurt, and I'm older. I'm supposed to protect you."

"Older by a breath and a push doesn't count," she said. "Talk to me, Eloise. I don't like not sharing your thoughts."

"And I don't like you closing yourself off." I gently pulled my sister into a hug. "It's okay to cry, Kellen."

She hugged me in return.

"I couldn't imagine my life without you, Eloise. You are indeed the Cinder to my Snow."

I groaned and pulled back to look at her.

"I shouldn't have forgiven Carver. Those words hurt you too deeply."

She smiled.

"You forgave him because that's who you are. And the words only hurt because they are true. But I like being the way I am. I like pushing the pain aside. I don't like hurting. I don't like feeling alone or knowing that someday, eventually, everyone will leave me. Because that is just how life is meant to be lived. Leave me the protection of my cold heart, my Cinder. Don't burn it away with your love."

I could see the pain in my sister's eyes and her desperation to hold herself together. Nodding, I kissed her cheek.

"Now, tell me what upsets you so much that you think two full grown women can comfortably sleep on this narrow bed."

"I never thought it would be comfortable," I said with a small grin.

She stared at me, and I gave in with a sigh.

"I think the necklace killed Mother."

Kellen closed her eyes.

"I do too."

I should have known she'd noticed. We were far too similar in how we thought.

"The boy who delivered it was wearing the king's insignia, the same as Kaven. Now, with Judith missing..."

My sister opened her eyes and looked at me. In that moment, I saw my mother in her expression.

"Do not let your temper blind you from seeing all of the truth, not just part of it."

"What does that mean?"

She exhaled softly.

"Mother had secrets. I'm not sure what they were. But, they had something to do with our births. Haven't you ever wondered why we live here on the king's land?"

"Someone needs to watch for poachers and keep an eye on the retreat."

"Father is a businessman. A merchant. He isn't a groundskeeper. And he pays Hugh to keep these grounds, not the king's."

"What are you saying?"

"That there might be more happening than we understand, and acting rashly out of some misguided attempt at retribution could see us torn apart."

Now, I understood. She'd known all along that Mother's death had been unnatural and had kept quiet because quiet was safe. It kept us safe.

Her fingers threaded through mine.

"You promised," she said softly. "Forever."

With Judith's absence looming in my mind, I nodded slowly, fearing my promise would be our undoing.

"I will search no more."

"Thank you."

I TOOK my time reading the spines of the books, looking for a title that sounded interesting. When I found an intriguing one, I plucked it from the shelf and opened to the first page.

"There needs to be a better way to determine what a book is about," Kellen said, snapping hers closed.

"Ask Mr. Bentwell," I said with a smirk. "He knows every book in here so well. He will tell you about them for hours if you asked."

"You're a horrible sister," Kellen said without any rancor.

My grin widened.

"Is there anything I can help you ladies find?" Mr. Bentwell called from his desk in the corner.

"No, thank you, Mr. Bentwell," Kellen said with a gracious smile. "We do so enjoy browsing the selection on our own. One never knows what will inspire the mind."

I had to turn my back to hide my mirth. She'd used his own quote against him. The scholar loved his books. He lent them out for a coin or two to those who had earned his trust. Mother first introduced us to Mr. Bentwell years ago when Kellen and I were still missing our front teeth and just learning our letters. Back when Mother still left the house occasionally.

My humor faded, and I closed the book.

"Actually, Mr. Bentwell," I said turning, "I could use your guidance. Grief eats at me, and I wish to escape to another place. Somewhere happier. Lighter. Can you recommend such a book?"

He looked at me with an understanding light in his eyes.

"I have just such a book about a maid who frees a man from a curse. It's not commonly borrowed, which is a shame. It's a lovely book with pretty drawings."

He stood from his desk and shuffled toward the shelves just to his right where he kept his favorite volumes. Neither Kellen nor I usually browse there for fear of a lengthy conversation. Today, a distraction was just what I needed, though.

Judith had never returned yesterday. Or this morning. Seeing Mother die had been a blow I never wished to repeat. Yet, the ignorance of Judith's fate continued to wear at me, unraveling my thoughts and creating a deeper grief that restlessly prodded my imagination to conjure every possible demise she might have met.

Mr. Bentwell suddenly plucked a tome from the shelves, jarring me from the darkening spiral of my thoughts.

"Here you are," he said. "I was terribly aggrieved to

hear of your mother's passing. Please accept my sympathies." He plucked another volume from his shelf and handed it to me. "Give this one to your sister. I hope I'll see both of you again soon."

And with that, we were summarily dismissed from his shop.

Kellen hooked her arm through mine and tugged me away, likely before Mr. Bentwell could change his mind and start talking.

"He's sweet," I said when the door closed behind us.

"He is," she agreed.

We walked for a time toward the market.

"I hate town," Kellen said. "But I find I have no desire to return home, either. I'm a person without a proper place."

I briefly set my head on her shoulder, not an easy task given her four-inch height deficiency.

"I feel the same. These books will help. I do think we should also look at the paints. We have too much idle time on our hands. Our minds need distraction," I said, quoting our mother.

"Painting is a far more sensible suggestion than gatherings and cakes," she said, patting my head before lightly pushing me away.

I grinned just as Alfie stepped from the shadows. He froze when he saw us. We did the same.

For a moment, his eyes narrowed, and I wondered how I would ever explain a damaged book's spine to Mr. Bentwell when Alfie's expression cleared.

"I have no intention of courting either of you," he said with barely concealed anger. "My actions weren't some concealed attraction. I don't like you. It's that simple."

"Look, Kellen. Asses truly can speak. I can't say it's an improvement over the braying, though."

"I quite agree," Kellen said.

Instead of bristling, Alfie gave us a shallow bow.

"I shall do my best to avoid you shrews and would appreciate the same courtesy."

"With pleasure," I said.

He turned on his heel and stomped away.

"Why is it he doesn't like us?" I asked.

"It was probably that time you—"

"Don't say it," I said, remembering.

"—spit the ale in his face in front of his friends."

I shook my head. Kellen and I had snuck away from Mother during one of our jaunts into town and wandered too close to Alfie's family alehouse. I'd just picked up a discarded tankard curious to taste what everyone was drinking when Kellen had whispered in my ear, "What if it's cat piss?"

My sister's pranks, while entertaining, often saw me in trouble. However, that time, the prank had doomed both of us. Those words and Alfie's unfortunate timing had apparently sealed a lifelong hatred.

"I couldn't have timed that better if I had tried," she said.

"I'm still of a mind that you had tried."

She grinned, showing a rare glimpse of humor, and we made our way back to the wagon where Hugh waited.

"Finished?" he asked, his gaze missing its usual humor.

"Yes," Kellen said, settling onto the seat beside him.

The ride home was swift and quiet under grey skies. I'd hoped to read outside to avoid whichever guest Maeve entertained in the sitting room; however, rain started to fall just as the wagon rolled into the yard. Kellen and I held the books to our chests and ran for the kitchen door.

Anne looked up from her place by the fire. She'd been sitting quietly, staring into the flames.

"I've been thinking," she said. "What if Judith went to her family?"

Kellen and I shared a glance. Judith would have said something, not just up and left. However, Anne, like the rest of us, was struggling to understand what had happened to Judith. We all needed answers.

"Perhaps," Kellen said. "It's a few hours ride, correct?"

Anne nodded.

"We can send Hugh to check," I said, setting my book on the table.

I left the kitchen, pulling up my hood to run through the light rain to the shed where Hugh stayed. Barely inside the doors, I heard something. It was like a thump of flesh against something. I frowned and slowed my steps, wondering if I should retreat or announce my presence. I did neither.

Creeping forward, I peered through the cracks between

the boards separating Hugh's quarters from the carriage house. I saw Hugh hitting a post repeatedly. He stopped suddenly and hung his head.

"I need you. End my torment and return to me."

I covered my mouth in surprise. Judith had been close to my mother's age. Close to Maeve's age. Hugh was several years younger, nearer Kellen and me than Judith. I'd never considered that they might have had feelings for one another.

Retreating to the door, I called out for Hugh.

"Just a moment," he called back.

When he appeared, his anguish was well-hidden.

"Anne suggested that we check with Judith's family. Would you be willing to ride there today, despite the rain?"

"Have you spoken to Maeve about this?" he asked.

I shook my head.

"We still have a visitor. Please Hugh. Judith means so much to us all."

He ran a hand through his hair, and I saw his raw knuckles but didn't comment.

"The rain is likely to get heavier. As much as I want to go, it would be foolish to risk the horse if she truly is there. I will leave as soon as the weather clears. Please let Maeve know of our plans."

He turned and closed himself back inside his room. With a heavy heart, I ran to the house to share the news with the others. Hugh's love for Judith, I kept to myself.

CHAPTER NINE

"Don't be greedy," I said, scolding the fattest hen in the yard.

I threw more grain to the others and she ran to the new pile.

A sound from the shed drew my attention, and I watched as Hugh led out one of our horses. After two days of rain, I'd woken to peer out the window at a clear sky. Although dawn had barely been on the horizon, I'd rushed to dress and do my chores so I would be in the yard for Hugh's departure.

"Are you leaving, then?" I asked.

He nodded.

Shaking out my apron, I went to him as he mounted. The horse nuzzled into my palm, likely hoping for a treat, when I reached out to pet her nose.

"A safe journey to both of you," I said.

Hugh looked at the house for a moment before meeting my gaze.

"I will return before dinner." With that, he clucked to the horse, and the pair left the yard at a steady trot.

Chores finished, I returned to the house and crept back upstairs where Kellen still slept. We'd both stayed up far too late, reading by candlelight. She'd finished her book by the time the candle went out. I had a few more pages to mine and settled in to read. However, the story ended far too quickly, and I said farewell to the distraction. It had been a welcome one during the rain.

Closing the book, I watched my sister sleep and wondered what we would do today to keep ourselves occupied.

With Hugh gone, a ride into town for a new book wouldn't be feasible. Although there was another horse and Kellen and I both knew how to ride, I didn't think riding double while in our mourning garb would portray an image of which Maeve would approve.

"What are you thinking?" Kellen asked without opening her eyes.

"That I don't like when you do that."

She grinned lightly and looked at me.

"Did you finish your book?"

"Yes. I saw Hugh off this morning."

"Ah."

She rose for the day, and I accompanied her to the kitchen where we ate a quiet breakfast.

"I was thinking I would take the pig for a walk to hunt for more truffles," Anne said. "After all that rain, we should find a good amount. The mushrooms would go well in a stew with some of the venison in the cold storage."

"Are you sure?" I asked. "I can do it."

Anne shook her head.

"It would do me some good to leave the quiet of the kitchen."

We watched her take her cloak and walk out. The door had barely closed when the one leading to the dining room opened.

"Good morning, girls," Maeve said. She went straight to the board and took the egg Anne had waiting for her. "Did you sleep well? I thought I saw light from your room just before I fell asleep."

"We stayed up late reading," Kellen said. "The story was too intriguing to put aside."

Maeve smiled as she joined us.

"I do love a good story. Do you plan to return to town today for another?"

"Hugh left this morning," I said.

"I see. Tomorrow, then," she said with a kind smile. "Where is Anne this morning?"

"She took the pig for a walk. She's looking for truffles."

Maeve frowned.

"Alone?"

I felt my stomach dip and glanced at Kellen. Why hadn't we thought of that?

"The pig is quite large and much slower than Anne. If something is out there looking for a feast, I'm sure it will be the pig and not Anne who suffers," Kellen said, taking my hand and giving it an encouraging squeeze.

"I'm sure you're right," Maeve said. "Forget I said anything."

Outside, we heard the sound of a carriage. Maeve sighed and pushed aside her half-eaten egg.

"I will see you two at dinner. If you need me, you know where I'll be."

I nodded and watched her go.

"Do you think we should help her today?" I asked.

"Help her to do what? She's more skilled at social niceties than we are. If we went in there, we'd likely say something that would give the gossips exactly what they want."

I knew Kellen was right but still felt bad that Maeve had to speak with every unwelcomed busybody who lived in the kingdom of Drisdall.

"I think I'm going to retreat to the attic today," Kellen said, throwing her egg shell into the fire. "What are you going to do?"

I shrugged.

"I'll find something."

As soon as the door closed behind her, I grabbed my cloak and rushed outside. The tracks from the pig were easy to follow from the yard. Because of the rain, my portly friend left deep pits in the earth with each step.

I caught up with Anne on the other side of Mother's grave. The pig was rooting around on his tether, and Anne was looking up at the sky. The peace on her face begged for solitude. So, I kept my distance and did not intrude.

The distant baying of hounds interrupted the silence of the woods several times before she had a healthy pile of mushrooms in her little basket.

"Come, pig," she said. "Let's return you to your pen."

I followed her through the trees but stopped at Mother's grave, letting Anne continue home on her own.

With the plentiful rain, the pear tree had grown again. Far too much to be natural, though. It reached the height of my head and had branches the length of my arms. When I sat on the bench to study it, a small, darkly colored bird landed on one of the thin branches.

"What do you think of the tree?" I asked it. The bird chirped back at me, singing a pretty song. I listened for a while and thought of Mother.

When the song finished, I thanked the bird.

"Will you sing for her again tomorrow even if I'm not here?"

It took flight, roosting in a larger tree not far away.

"I hope that's a yes." I sighed and looked at the dirt covering Mother's grave. The rain and time had reduced the height of the mound. It looked barely more than a small bump now. Little shoots of green were sprouting from the ground, nothing growing as vigorously as the pear tree.

I stood and touched one of the branches.

"Watch over her. Keep what's left of her safe."

When I returned to the kitchen, the truffles were on the board, and the kitchen was empty. Voices echoed from the sitting room. With nothing else to do, I went in search of Kellen and found her in the attic, reading a letter.

"Haven't you read them all yet?"

"Twice actually."

"Then let's walk to town. Maeve is with a visitor, and there's nothing else to do."

"We'll take something to carry more than one book home this time," she said, standing.

The pair of us slipped past the sitting room and paused in the kitchen.

"We should leave a note so no one worries," Kellen said. It wasn't easy finding a slip of parchment for an idle note. It required more sneaking past the sitting room door to get to Father's study.

"How much can one woman need to say?" I said softly to Kellen. "First, it was her daughter's marriage, and now it's her husband's business ventures."

"Talking about one's success makes one feel more important," Kellen said when the kitchen door closed behind us.

"Bragging isn't becoming."

"Based on her lack of comment, I'm certain Maeve hears it for what it is."

We scrawled a quick note and left it on the block by the truffles.

The day was warming and the walk to town pleasant.

"Have you given our lives as liberated women of travel any further thought?" I asked Kellen when we reached the outskirts.

"Not really."

"Why not? I'm entirely serious."

"Which is why I don't need to give it thought. You have a way of making things happen, Eloise. If you want us to travel the world, we will. Thought on my part isn't necessary."

I huffed a breath.

"Of course it is. I need to know where you want to travel."

A small smile tugged at her lips at the sign of my exasperation. She enjoyed my flare for emotion even as she kept hers in check.

"I would love to see the snow in the north. I heard it can become so deep a woman can't walk in it with skirts. Pants are necessary."

I paused to look at her.

"Women wearing pants?"

She nodded, her smile growing.

"I can't tell if you're being serious now or not."

She laughed which made me think the latter.

"Fine. We shall travel to the north, and I will see for

myself if there are indeed women wearing pants in order to walk through the snow."

We reached Mr. Bentwell's shop and let ourselves in. This time, instead of quietly browsing in hopes of avoiding a conversation, I tugged Kellen right up to his desk.

"Eloise and Kellen Cartwright," he said with a welcoming smile. "I didn't think I would see you again so soon."

"We devoured these books," I said, removing the books in question from the bag. "Would you have any others like them? Perhaps by the same authors?"

He chuckled.

"I do have several others that I think you'll like if those struck your fancy."

He stood and shuffled toward his prized shelves, sliding the books back into place before selecting new ones.

"Could we perhaps borrow two each this time?" Kellen asked.

"You've been bitten by the book bug, I see," he said. Without hesitation, he took two more from the shelves. "These will suit you, Kellen." He handed her two thick tomes. "And these will suit you, Eloise."

In no time, we were walking toward the market for a bite to eat.

"I should have read your book before returning it," I said. "This time, we should trade."

"If you wish."

We both inhaled deeply, catching the same scent.

Following our noses, we ordered two fresh meat pies and started home.

"What comes after we see the north?" I asked.

"I don't know. What do you want to see?"

I thought about it for a moment.

"Turre. Or maybe somewhere even further south. Somewhere magic isn't banned."

Kellen gave me a curious look.

"Why?"

"Have you seen the pear tree?" I asked.

"I have."

"That's not natural. I'm certain it's growing like that because of magic. Is it residual magic because of Mother's death or is it something else? So many of our questions would already be answered if we had even a basic understanding of magic, I think."

"I see."

"Not that I'm pursuing anything, just idly dreaming about how it would be nice to have an explanation of how these things happened."

She gave me a small smile.

"I wouldn't mind knowing more, either. North then south it is. Perhaps we then go west before we return home to the east."

We idled away the distance with speculation over what we might see and learn and do in each area of our travels. When we reached the lane to our house, I noted fresh tracks and pointed them out to Kellen.

"One muddy rut looks like the other," she said with a shrug. "Do not get your hopes up that we will have a quiet house."

We passed the trees protecting the drive, and I groaned when I saw a second carriage had joined the first.

"It looks like you were right," Kellen said. "Those tracks were fresh."

We entered through the kitchen and set our books on the table.

"The note's still here," Kellen said, looking at the block.

The truffles hadn't moved either.

Before I had time to worry, the murmur of voices reached our ears. I moved to the dining room door and pushed it ajar enough to hear Maeve thank our guests and wish them a speedy journey.

I motioned to Kellen, and she stepped into the hall the moment the door closed.

"Have you seen Anne?" Maeve asked. "She didn't bring in tea or answer the door. I'm worried she didn't return from her walk."

"She returned," Kellen said. "There are truffles on the block."

Maeve's gaze grew more concerned.

"Has Hugh arrived?"

"I'm not certain," I said. "We just returned from town. We went for more books."

"Let us not worry just yet," Maeve said, gently herding us toward the kitchen. "I'll fix us some tea, and we'll wait for Anne. If she doesn't return by the time Hugh does, we will go look for her."

In the kitchen, Kellen found us something to eat while I made tea and Maeve paced. She checked the window constantly until I heard a soft, "about time." Opening the door, Maeve strode out.

Kellen and I followed and saw Hugh riding into the yard. Maeve hurried to his side.

"Anne's missing," she said. "You must find her. Check the woods."

He stared at Maeve for a long moment before nodding and sliding off the horse.

"We should split up," I said. "While there's still daylight."

Maeve shook her head.

"No. Hugh will look, and we will stay in the house."

"Four sets of eyes will cover more ground than one," I insisted.

Maeve came to me and took my hand in hers.

"Two people have already gone missing. I will not lose either of you."

While I understood her concern, I couldn't let fear of my own well-being stop me from helping someone I cared about. I glanced at Hugh, who was taking the saddle from the horse, and saw my chance.

"I understand," I said to Maeve. "Hugh, can I unsaddle Sugar for you? There's too little light left to waste."

Maeve released me as he nodded and started for the trees.

"Kellen, Anne will likely be chilled and hungry when she returns. Can you make something for dinner?" I asked.

"Of course," she said, already turning to the door.

Without looking at Maeve, I went to the horse.

"I'll brush you down, sweet thing," I crooned taking the reins. "You must be hot and tired from the long journey." I led her to the trough where she drank her fill. When she was done, I looked at the yard and saw it empty.

"Sorry, girl," I said softly, leading her into the stall. "A brushing will need to wait. Anne needs to be found before dark, and one man alone will not be enough."

I left her in the barn and snuck around the back to the woods. A familiar, low distant whistle echoed in the trees. The tune was one I'd often overheard when Hugh worked alone. I paused for a moment, trying to determine where he was and decided he was searching the area closest to the house.

Walking softly, I started down the path toward Mother's grave and listened carefully. The sound grew more distant, confirming my guess about Hugh's location. Nothing else moved once the whistle faded. The sound of my own passing and my gentle breathing kept me company as I watched the ground.

I saw my footprints and Anne's coming and going. Nothing else. My gaze swept the trees, my skin prickling. I felt watched. Halting, I turned a slow circle and saw nothing but the fading light of day.

Shaking off the feeling, I continued forward until I reached the clearing.

A bit of white against the new green robbed me of my hope. Woodenly, I walked forward and picked up Anne's cap. It hadn't been here this morning. That meant she'd returned to this spot after I'd watched her go to the house. Like Judith, Anne had disappeared.

"It's an odd tree, isn't it?" a voice said behind me.

I whirled to face Kaven. He was standing not far from me, facing my mother's grave and the pear tree.

"Where did you come from?" I demanded. "Why are you here?"

"Interesting questions coming from the girl who likes to lean against trees and watch other people."

He'd seen me but never acknowledged my presence? Why? Pulse racing, I stared at him, unsure and waiting for what he would do next.

"Nothing to say?" he asked, glancing at me before resuming his study of the tree. "It's growing much too quickly. Almost as if by magic."

He turned to face me and glanced at the cap in my hands.

"That doesn't belong to you."

My insides started to quake with rage. He knew and was baiting me. All of it. Mother's death by magic...the disappearances of our housemaids. After the delivery boy,

Kaven had been in the woods. The same woods where people now disappeared. And, he'd been wearing the same hat as the boy.

Words piled in my mouth, choking me as I held my tongue. This man wasn't the King, only a representative. Yet, I couldn't accuse him. Not without proof when anything he said would likely hold more weight to the King than anything I could say.

"Last time we met, you had plenty to say," he said, stalking closer to me.

The deep blue of his gaze bore into mine. I raged at him. He'd taken so much. No more.

"Speak now, Eloise," he said when he towered over me. "Save yourself."

While meeting his gaze, I tugged back my long skirts and sharply lifted my knee. The connection to his groin was solid and true. With a grunt, his face reddened then paled as he cupped his testicles and slowly fell over.

I leaned over him, knowing I had several moments.

"I will see you hanged for what you've done," I said harshly. "I swear it on my mother's name, I will see you—"

Something caught my ankle, and I suddenly found myself on my back with a very angry man pinning me down. A vein throbbed in his forehead as his bloodshot gaze found mine.

"Pray, what have I done to deserve that?"

Each pain-laced word fell on my deaf ears. The thrumming of my heart and the certainty of my own demise robbed me of thought as my hand searched the ground for what I knew was nearby. My fingers closed over a rock, and I immediately brought it down on Kaven's head.

The man slumped on top of me.

Fear, and a frantic amount of wiggling, saw me free of his weight and running toward the house. It wasn't until I'd almost reached the door that I realized I'd dropped Anne's cap. I halted and looked back.

Kaven stood near a tree, leaning on it heavily, watching me. Our gazes locked across the distance. He held up the cap then turned and disappeared into the trees.

CHAPTER TEN

KELLEN WAS IN THE KITCHEN WHEN I RETURNED SHAKEN AND muddy. I washed and said nothing about what had happened even though I saw the question in her gaze. When I was changed, I returned to the kitchen to help her with dinner.

Maeve joined us at the table. We'd just served ourselves when Hugh entered.

"I didn't find any sign of Anne," he said.

And still, I said nothing. What could I say without damning myself or Kellen in some way? I felt certain it was magic that killed Mother. That both Judith and Anne went missing less than a fortnight later couldn't be coincidence. Something was happening here. But what? It most certainly had to be tied to Kaven and the Crown. However, if I started crying magic, the king's men would descend, and it would be the remnants of my family who would suffer.

I looked at Kellen and found her watching me. I could almost hear her thoughts reminding me what I'd promised her. Bowing my head, I stared at the stew in my bowl.

"Thank you for looking, Hugh," Maeve said. "Join us."

Hugh usually never ate in the house, preferring to take his meals alone. However, this time he agreed. Kellen fetched him a bowl of stew and placed it on the opposite end of the table from Maeve.

Four people at the table. Just as it had been before Mother died. Yet, everything was different. I tried not to think about it and took a bite of the stew.

"I don't want you in the woods alone anymore," Maeve said after a moment of quiet eating. "I promised your father that I would keep you safe. I do not intend to break my word. It's too dangerous out there."

I nodded in quiet agreement. The woods were far too dangerous with Kaven lurking about.

After dinner, Kellen and I retreated to our room. She watched me close the door and sat on the edge of her bed. Of course she'd known I wouldn't brush the horse.

In a hushed voice, I told her what had transpired. The cap. Kaven's sudden appearance. My narrow escape.

"I want to ignore it," Kellen said. "To turn away and let someone else deal with this, but you're right. Mother, Judith, and now Anne. I don't believe this will stop."

"I agree. But what are we supposed to do? How are we supposed to stop this?"

"Perhaps we should speak with Maeve."

I shook my head.

"I did speak to her of my suspicions. Her opinion is the same as yours. That we cannot say anything for fear of being persecuted ourselves."

"Then, what do you suggest?"

"We now know that Kaven is involved. The messenger might have been unaware of the purpose for his delivery. The only part I'm uncertain about is the backing of the Crown. If the king knows of this, no amount of proof will save us."

"Then we run," Kellen said.

"How will we convince Maeve to—"

"No, Eloise. We run."

I nodded.

"All right. But, first, we try to find out if Kaven's actions are his own or that of the King's."

"Agreed."

As I lay in bed that night, my mind raced regarding how I could possibly determine the Crown's involvement. It wasn't until the sliver of the moon was high, its weak light shining through the window, that a fitful slumber claimed me.

When the sun rose, I was dressed and ready. This time, I was the one to poke my sister in the eye.

She groaned and rolled to her back before looking up

at me.

"Why must you always wake so early?"

"I have a plan," I said quietly.

She sat up, her dark braid falling over her shoulder to her waist.

"Tell me."

I sat on the edge of her bed so we were close.

"We need to check the inside of the retreat for signs of magic. If we find some, we can anonymously—"

The soft knock on our door caused us both to jump. Kellen's gaze locked with mine for a moment. We would speak later. I went to answer the knock.

Maeve waited in the hall, already dressed for the day.

"Good morning. I'm glad you're already awake. Is Kellen? May I speak with you both?"

I opened the door wider and invited her in.

She smiled good morning to Kellen then began to pace the small confines of our room.

"We have a problem we can no longer keep to ourselves," she began. "We need to report the mysterious disappearances. Yet, I worry how such a thing will reflect on this household, and more importantly, the pair of you. In addition to reporting Judith and Anne missing, we will be challenged with finding replacements." She held up her hands as if to forestall any argument from us. "These replacements need not be permanent. If, no, when Judith and Anne return, of course they will be welcomed back. But, with the visitors and the rumors of the king's impending visit, we need help."

"I agree," Kellen said. "However, we need to be discreet in reporting the issue or it will make finding new help harder."

Maeve's expression turned grateful, and she exhaled hugely.

"I was so worried you would think ill of me for suggesting that we bring in others to work."

"Not at all," I said.

"It is the only practical course of action," Kellen agreed.

"Very good. Then, I'd like you both to dress and accompany Hugh and me to town. I cannot leave you home alone. Not with..." She shook her head.

"We'll be down in a few minutes," Kellen said.

I closed the door after Maeve left and shared a look with Kellen.

"It would be ideal to check the retreat while they're gone," I said.

Kellen shook her head and started to change.

"I disagree. If we find something and need assistance, we would be alone. Best to wait until we return. Besides, going to town can benefit us."

"In what way?"

"We might be able to learn what the king is up to and why the retreat is being prepared. All this trouble started with that, did it not?"

I agreed and willingly followed her down the stairs.

The trip to town didn't take long in the comfort of the carriage. And this time, we didn't need to cover our noses. Only a hint of dank and damp remained.

"I've asked Hugh to stop near the market so you can shop while we're here. I would prefer you not be present when I speak with the king's guard. The conversation will likely be upsetting, and I wouldn't put you through that. When I've finished, Hugh and I will return and find you."

Since Maeve's plan aligned with our goals, Kellen and I quickly agreed and found ourselves walking the market district with the early morning crowd.

"You know there's only one place to go for this kind of gossip," Kellen said.

"Try not to make me spit my ale this time."

We made our way to Alfie's family alehouse and found a table near the window. This close to the market district, Crumbs and Casks maintained a respectability most alehouses did not. A serving girl came to offer us a drink and some breakfast.

"Have you heard anything about the king retiring to his hunting retreat soon?" Kellen asked before the girl could leave.

"Not a thing. It wouldn't make sense for him to go there now, what with his son due back and all that."

"The prodigal prince is returning?" I asked in disbelief.

The girl nodded. "I heard that he found himself a wife during his time away. Some Lord's daughter from the far north. I'm excited to see what style of dresses the gentry will start wearing, trying to impress the girl."

"What if she wears pants?" Kellen asked. "I heard that the women wear pants that far north."

The serving girl looked intrigued before Alfie's father called her name and she hurried away.

"I wonder if Kaven is really there on behalf of the king, then," Kellen said softly.

"What we need is information from a source that is more likely to know the king's intentions."

"No one within the king's inner circle would ever consider sharing that information with the likes of us."

"The king's inner circle aren't the only ones privy to the comings and goings of the royal family."

"The king's guard? They would never speak to us about such matters, either."

She was right, but I still regretted not being with Maeve at the moment. Maybe Kellen and I would have overheard something.

Kellen's eyes lit up.

"You know who may know something?"

"Who?"

"The dressmaker. These guards have wives, don't they? Husbands confide in wives, and a good many wives love to gossip."

"Perfect. And we must stop in to check on our dresses," I said with a grin.

After we finished our meal, we left the alehouse and

made our way to Madame Todd's. She wasn't surprised to see us and immediately showed us to the back rooms for a fitting.

"Your timing is impeccable," she said. "We just finished your gowns last night."

The dresses she produced were beautiful with the exception of all the black material. Kellen and I changed and stood in our positions for the hemming.

"Have you heard anything about the king retiring to his hunting retreat soon?" Kellen asked again.

"Not the king but the prince," one of the seamstresses said. "It would seem he's not yet ready to return to palace life and wants the solitude of the retreat."

"And his wife is okay with living in the woods?" Kellen asked.

"So it would seem," another said. "Not much is known about his wife."

"Other than she comes from the north, correct?" I said.

The girl nodded.

"I hear the women wear pants in the north," Kellen added. She was good at directing the conversation to keep the appearance of idle gossip.

They continued to share unimportant tidbits, such as the length of time the prince had been away, which we all knew; and the fact that the King was impatient for his son's return so the next generation might produce an heir. Again, more common knowledge.

"Perhaps that's the reason for the retreat," Kellen said,

making my jaw drop. She laughed at me. "What? Mr. Bentwell's book collection includes some romantic pieces, too."

That set the girls giggling, and a few vowed to visit Mr. Bentwell.

When we were finished, they wrapped the gowns then led us out to the waiting room. Luck was on our side that we'd only just left with our heavy packages when we spotted Maeve walking toward us.

She smiled in greeting. "I'm so glad you remembered the gowns. It completely slipped my mind. Come, we had better return to the estate. With no one there to answer the door and turn visitors away, the gossips are sure to speculate on what is happening."

We followed her back the way she'd come.

"It's understandable you forgot," Kellen said. "You've been dealing with so much for us."

"The dresses are lovely," I added. "Thank you for selecting them."

Maeve smiled back at us.

"It was no trouble. I hope you didn't need to stand too long to get them fitted."

"Not too long," I said.

"The girls distracted us with conversation," Kellen added as we reached the carriage.

"Oh? Anything interesting?" Maeve asked, letting us enter first.

Kellen was dying to share the news just as much as I,

but I was faster as we settled into the carriage for the journey home.

"It's not the king who's coming to the retreat but the prince and his new wife," I said.

Maeve gave us an indecipherable look before smiling kindly.

"Yes, I just heard the same at the guard house."

"Did they offer any help in finding Judith and Anne?" Kellen asked.

"Unfortunately, two housemaids do not warrant their attention. If someone of more note goes missing in the same manner, then perhaps the guard will be interested. Until then..." She lifted a shoulder and looked out the window, visibly upset.

The rest of the carriage ride was made in silence. When we stopped before our stable, we saw a carriage already waiting in the yard.

"Drat and bother," Maeve said under her breath.

"I'll fix some tea and bring it in to you," Kellen said.

"No. You can't be seen serving tea. But if you're willing to fix it and leave it in the dining room, I'll gladly fetch it from there."

Hugh helped Maeve down then took our packages into the kitchen while Maeve went directly to the visitors. We waited until everyone was inside before sneaking into the house through the kitchen door.

Hugh stood by the hearth, looking at the flames.

"Are you all right?" I asked softly.

"No. I feel so empty inside. Don't leave the house."

He turned and strode out. Both Kellen and I watched after him.

"He seems odd," Kellen said after a moment.

"I think he was in love with Judith."

Kellen looked at me, her brows high.

"Why do you think that?"

"I saw him hitting a post after he couldn't find her. And heard him say he felt empty without her."

"Poor Hugh," she said, her expression changing to one of pity before carefully clearing.

I knew how she felt. If she let pity in, she'd open herself to all the other emotions waiting to take control. Yet, closing herself off wasn't going to help her deal with the drastic changes that continued occurring in our lives.

"Is it ever going to get better for us?" I asked.

Kellen came and wrapped her arms around me.

"Don't give up hope. Not you, Eloise."

I hugged her in return.

"I'm trying not to. I just can't bear the thought that Judith and Anne might be lost to us for good."

"I know. But remember, we can't change what's already happened. We can only steer the course for our future."

I nodded and helped make the tea. When we were finished, we left the tray in the dining room before returning to the kitchen. Without speaking, we grabbed our cloaks and slipped out the door, ignoring Hugh's protective warning.

The walk through the woods was peaceful. Birds chirped, and small animals chittered at us from still barren branches.

"It's starting to smell like spring," Kellen said quietly.

I inhaled deeply, loving the smell.

A soft sound drew our attention. We paused and listened. I pointed to our right but motioned for Kellen to continue to follow me in the direction in which we'd been headed. Circling around, I spotted Kaven through the trees and stopped Kellen from going any further. He'd obviously noted my presence before, and I didn't want to risk him coming after me...us...again.

Bow gripped in his hand, he had his head tipped up to the sky. As I watched, he lifted the bow and rapidly fired two arrows with barely a glance before looking at the sky again.

Even from this distance, I could see the rage in his stance.

"Where are you?" he roared, scaring the birds and setting my heart hammering.

Motioning to Kellen, we backed away. But not toward home. Once he was out of sight, I lifted my skirts and hurried toward the retreat. Who knew how much time we had before he returned there?

Neither Kellen nor I spoke when the king's lodge came into view. She followed me to the back where I tried the door and found it locked. I looked at the stone work and started tying my skirts together.

"Are you sure?" Kellen whispered.

I nodded.

"Hide in the shrubs and call if he comes. I'll leave through the same window."

She moved back to stand watch as I used the stones to climb to a second story window. My fingers grew numb in moments from the damp and the cold on the rock, and my feet slipped twice. But I'd fallen that height before and knew it wouldn't hurt. Much.

Bracing my weight on my forearm, I used my other hand to push at the window and was rewarded when it swung inward without a sound. My muscles protested as I hauled myself over the ledge, but I made it.

Standing carefully, I looked around at the bedroom. Well-stuffed bed. Neat linens. Dust free baseboards. No cobwebs on the ceiling. A room meant for the royal family, then.

On light feet, I crept down the hall and peeked into each room. I wasn't sure what evidence of a murder or magic would look like, but I felt certain I would know it when I saw it.

In a room at the far end of the hall, I found a multitude of covered furniture and other items. Some of them looked familiar, and I realized they were the ones I saw unloaded from the wagons. I frowned as I studied the number. So many things to be unloaded then shoved away for storage. Why not air them in preparation? Unless, perhaps, the prince and his wife's arrival was delayed or unknown. That would be an explanation for Kaven's anger just now.

I lifted the cover from a few pieces and admired the pretty floral designs. After finding a box with lavish jewels, it became obvious that all of the items belonged to the princess. Tucking the box away, I moved to leave. A partially exposed painting behind the door caught my eye. It was a woman's bare shoulder.

Creeping closer, I pulled back the oil-cover and stared at a young woman who looked very similar to me. Her blue eyes seemed to lock with mine as I studied the blonde hair piled high on her head and threaded with ribbon to match the green of her dress. The painter had perfectly blushed her cheeks. Yet, she lacked life. She looked tired.

And I knew why.

A familiar green amulet lay nestled on her breast. A glint of light reflected on the stone, hinting at an unnatural life I knew it possessed.

Kellen's soft dove call reached my ears, and I hurried to cover the painting. Racing down the hall, I made it back to the bedroom when I heard the front door open.

Kellen was below, motioning for me to hurry. I didn't hesitate to throw my leg over the ledge and start my descent, not wasting time to close the window. I dropped the last few feet and took off at a run, trusting my sister to keep up with me.

We didn't stop until we reached the clearing where we collapsed in a heap on the bench beside Mother's grave.

"Did you find anything?" she asked, her breathing ragged but her voice soft.

"A picture of a woman wearing the same necklace as the one delivered to Mother."

"Was the King in the picture? Or the Prince?"

I shook my head. "Only her."

She sighed, and I understood why. A woman wearing the same necklace wasn't the evidence we needed, but clearly Mother's death was linked to the royal family. I wanted to rage and kick something. However, the sudden baying of hounds warned me I didn't have the time to lose my temper.

"We need to get inside," I said, grabbing Kellen's hand.

It wasn't until the kitchen door was firmly closed behind us that I breathed a little easier.

"What will prevent Kaven from coming here?" she asked.

"Nothing, but I don't think he will. Whatever he has planned, I believe he needs to remain hidden for a while longer. If he was ready to strike, we would be with Judith and Anne right now."

"You believe he's acting on his own then?"

"If he doesn't come pounding on our door, yes."

Kellen considered me for a moment and nodded.

"Let's start dinner."

Maeve found us in the kitchen an hour later.

"Mrs. Wineford just left," she said. "Thank you both for

the tray and for preparing dinner. Tomorrow, we'll return to town to search for help."

"Perhaps, instead of all of us going, I can go with Hugh," I said. "That way, someone will be here to answer the door."

She considered me.

"Are you sure? Hiring kitchen help might not be easy."

"I'm sure. You're doing so much for us already while Kellen and I sit idle."

She waved away the comment and joined us at the table.

"Really, I'm doing very little but deflecting unwanted questions and listening to frivolous gossip for hours on end."

"I think we need to start setting aside certain hours for people to call," Kellen said. "Our new help can turn visitors away on our behalf and let them know the appropriate hours to call again. As you said, with royalty soon to be in residence at the retreat, the rush of visitors will only grow."

Maeve's expression lit up.

"That is a marvelous idea. It would free up my time so I can attend to other neglected matters. I have no idea what the expenses are for the estate or any repairs that might be needed. I should probably speak with Hugh after dinner."

"I can fix a plate for you to take to him."

"That's a lovely idea. We need him to keep his strength for us during these trying times."

CHAPTER ELEVEN

"ARE YOU FEELING WELL?" I ASKED HUGH.

His pallor seemed a little ashen in the morning light. Perhaps it was the jostle of the wagon on an empty stomach.

"I'm fine. Please stay close to me today. Maeve is worried you'll find trouble."

"Trouble? Me?" I grinned because he knew me well. He didn't grin back.

My humor died at the absence of his. I knew why he was so subdued. No matter how much I tried to tell myself that Judith was somewhere else, alive and well, I knew it was a lie. My heart wanted to break. Judith had been like a second mother to Kellen and me. Stern when we were trouble, loving when we needed comfort. But most importantly, always there.

"I miss her so much," I said.

"Don't talk like that," Hugh said gruffly.

I nodded and looked away so he wouldn't see the start of my tears, which I fought to blink back. He was right. I couldn't think like that. There had to be hope.

We traveled the rest of the way to town in silence, and Hugh parked the wagon not far from the market district.

"Where do you want to start?" he asked.

"I was thinking of ordering some breakfast at Crumbs and Casks and asking the serving girl if she knows of anyone who might be looking for kitchen work."

He grunted his acknowledgment and followed me down the street. When it came time to order, he left me at my own table and moved off to the bar. I didn't mind. It would be odd for an employee to be seated with me.

Along with a delicious meal, the serving girl gave me a few names and directions for finding the women. Hugh forestalled me from searching them out, though.

"First, I need to deliver a message to the Brazen Belle," he said. "The staff should be awake by now."

The name struck a familiar chord, and I didn't remember why until I saw a face I recognized. The old woman from the woods was sitting in the sunlight on the porch while shucking some peas. She didn't glance our way as we approached.

"Stay right here," Hugh said, stopping me from stepping onto the porch. "This is no place for a young miss."

I nodded and watched him go inside. The old woman winked at me and tossed me a pea.

"How's the pig?" she asked as I munched on the sweet green.

"Still big. But he seems happy enough."

The woman snorted.

"If he's happy enough, it means you're feeding him too much. Cut the portions. Are you walking him?"

"Yes, ma'am."

"Is he finding anything for you?"

"Truffles."

She cackled and slapped her knee.

"He would have a good nose that one. Tell him that's not good enough. He can do better."

I nodded just as Hugh returned.

He glanced suspiciously at the old woman.

"What were you telling her?"

"We were talking about the pig," I said to Hugh.

He came down the steps, grabbed my arm, and led me away.

"You aren't supposed to speak with the women there," he said.

"Was that a whorehouse?" I asked, my curiosity piqued. Behind us, the old woman laughed again, and Hugh lengthened his stride, his face reddening.

"I promise, Hugh. We were strictly discussing the pig. I wasn't educated in any way." I eased my arm from his grasp and patted his shoulder. "Besides, the woman is harmless and hardly a whore, given her age."

He gave a quick side-glance and seemed to relax a little.

"Before we visit the women the serving girl mentioned, I have a stop I'd like to make," I said.

Hugh followed me through the winding roads of Towdown toward the center of the city. The palace was just barely visible above the rooftops when I saw the home I needed.

"How much further are we going?" Hugh asked. "I think we've been gone too long. We don't want to worry Maeve."

"She won't be worried. She knows I'm with you," I said with a quick smiled. "Besides, the house we need is just there."

As I pointed, the door opened, and Anne's mother stepped out. I waved when she spotted us.

"We shouldn't be here," Hugh said.

"Nonsense. We need to ask after Anne."

He followed me, his growing nervousness clearly visible. I couldn't blame him. My stomach was in knots.

"Hello, Mrs. Tiller."

"Eloise, dear. I didn't expect to see you."

"I know. I apologize for coming unannounced, but I needed to know if you've seen Anne in the last few days?"

"No, but I know she'll visit when she has time. She loves your family. I was so sorry to hear about your mother, dear."

"Thank you, Mrs. Tiller." I swallowed hard, struggling with what I needed to say next. She noticed.

"What is it, dear?"

"I truly believe Anne loves us as much as we love her. That's why I'm here. She's missing."

"Missing?"

"I found her cap in the woods. Nothing else. Judith is missing, too."

Mrs. Tiller lifted her hand to her mouth. The color left her face, and her eyes started to water.

"We've searched the woods and notified the guard. I don't know where else to look. I'd hoped I would find her here," I finished sadly.

Mrs. Tiller remained quiet for a moment, her gaze unfocused. Then she shook her head, turned around, and went inside without another word.

"We shouldn't have come," Hugh said softly. "You've brought nothing but pain."

I wished Hugh was wrong. I'd desperately hoped that Mrs. Tiller had seen Anne.

"Come," Hugh said softly. "It's best if we leave searching for help for another day. We should return home."

Maeve had entrusted me with the task of returning with the help we desperately needed. Yet, while obligation urged me to disagree with Hugh's insistence we leave, I found myself nodding in agreement instead. After seeing Mrs. Tiller's devastated expression, I no longer had the resolve to bring more people into our home. Would we be heartlessly risking someone new without first determining the root of our problems? Lost in thought, I followed Hugh.

We'd only reached the market district when a commotion on one of the side streets caught my attention. A group of boys, some of them familiar to me, were surrounding another, smaller lad. I couldn't see what they were doing; but having been the center of such a circle before, I couldn't allow it to continue unchecked.

Without thought, I veered in that direction.

"Eloise," Hugh called.

"Just a moment," I said before calling to the boys. "You there! Stop pushing him."

The motley group broke a part and scattered in different directions. The little boy straightened, looked me in the eye, and placed what they'd been fighting over on his head.

My eyes widened at the sight of the cap with the king's insignia, and my gaze shifted to the lad's face. The delivery boy.

He turned and sprinted off in the opposite direction.

"Wait!" I lifted my skirts and bolted after him. I'd barely covered any distance when I was lifted off my feet and spun around.

I stared wide-eyed at Hugh's angry face.

"I told you to stay with me," he said.

"I know, but I need to—"

"Return home where you're safe. Will you listen, or must I carry you?"

I narrowed my eyes at him before catching myself. He didn't deserve to be a target for my temper. He was only worried about me, which I understood. Carefully masking my frustration, I promised to stay close, and Hugh released me.

My vexation still hadn't dissipated by the time we arrived at the wagon. It didn't ease during the ride home, either.

Maeve waited on the front step when we pulled into the yard. Her expression subtly changed to worry when she saw no one else accompanied us.

"Oh dear," she said, coming down the steps as I jumped from the wagon. "I feared it might not be an easy task. Has word already spread?" She looked to Hugh.

"It will now. Eloise spoke to Mrs. Tiller about Anne and Judith. Told her that she found Anne's cap in the woods." He looked down at the ground, his frustration and upset clear. I realized my slip, that only Kellen had known about the cap, and looked at Maeve.

She was visibly surprised.

"You should have told me, Eloise. Who is Mrs. Tiller?"

"Anne's mother," I said. "I rather hoped we'd find Anne there. That the cap I found in the woods meant nothing. Unfortunately, Mrs. Tiller said she hadn't seen Anne since well before her disappearance."

Pity clouded Maeve's features. There wasn't a hint of anger or admonishment that I hadn't confided in her.

"I never thought of Anne's mother," Maeve said. "I'm so

sorry that you had to speak with her, Eloise. I should go see her immediately. What a mess." She looked truly upset.

"I'm sure Mrs. Tiller would like to hear from you, especially to know that we haven't given up hope. But probably not today. I let her know that we spoke with the king's guard, but she was very upset and went inside without a word."

"I understand." She exhaled slowly and looked away for a moment. "Were there no candidates then for help?"

"I did get a few names. We were going to check them, but Hugh insisted we'd been gone too long."

She glanced at Hugh with a frown.

"She tried running off."

I rolled my eyes.

"Really, Hugh, you make me sound like an errant child. I heard a lad being terrorized by his peers and stepped to the side to put a stop it."

"Of course you're not a child," Maeve said soothingly. She hooked my arm and guided me toward the house, leaning in close so her next words were just for me. "I believe Hugh feels guilt for Judith and Anne's disappearances. He probably feels an even greater need to protect the rest of us now. Try not to fault him for that."

"I vow I don't. I truly do understand."

She patted my hand.

"I knew you would."

We went inside and joined Kellen in the sitting room

where she was reading one of Mr. Bentwell's books. She glanced at me, her expression changing as our gazes held.

"No guests?" I asked.

"No," Maeve said. "I let those who appeared know that we are now only accepting guests between ten and two so we can spend more time together in memory of your mother. I'm sure word is spreading quickly."

It felt good to know that Kellen and I wouldn't need to hide away the majority of the day anymore.

"Why don't you two read while I fix us something to eat?" Maeve suggested.

Kellen closed her book.

"We'll cook; you can look at the estate business. Eloise and I wouldn't know where to start with that."

Maeve smiled and moved off to the small writing desk where Mother and Judith used to go over household expenses. Kellen and I quietly left the room.

"What happened?" Kellen asked as soon as the kitchen door closed behind us.

"Your ability to read me is uncanny."

"You stared at me with an intensity equal to the pig's when you're about to feed him. It wasn't hard to deduce that you wanted to tell me something."

I laughed.

"You know me better than anyone."

"And no one will ever know me as well as you. Now tell me."

"I saw the boy who delivered the necklace."

She stopped slicing bread to stare at me. Her already pale skin paled further.

"You did?" she asked softly.

I nodded. "When I tried to chase him down, Hugh stopped me. But I know a few of the boys who were with him. Through them, I think I could find the boy. I just need to get to town without Hugh in tow."

Kellen considered me for a moment and exhaled heavily.

"You already have a plan, don't you?"

"Yes. I believe Hugh needs some tea with dinner," I said with a smile.

THE WORLD around me was full of night noises, the small sounds keeping me company on my ride into town. Kellen hadn't liked the idea of me going off on my own once everyone was abed. But I'd pointed out to her that both Judith and Anne disappeared during the day, and I also knew who to watch for.

However, she still wasn't fully convinced that Kaven was acting alone despite his frustration in the woods the day I'd snuck into the retreat and the fact that we'd not once run into anyone else. Neither of our beliefs could be proven without speaking to the lad who'd delivered the necklace, though. Thus, the necessity of my late-night ride.

While most of Towdown rested peacefully as I entered

town, a few establishments still welcomed customers. It was their rowdy enjoyment of abundant libations that would keep me safely unnoticed. Hopefully.

I'd tied my hair back and tucked it into my hood to hide the golden sheen that might attract unwanted attention. I'd also borrowed one of Judith's dresses. I knew she wouldn't mind. Not when doing so was meant to help find both her and Anne. No one would question a woman of lower class going to an alehouse for a late meal.

Dismounting near the smith, I gave the boy there a coin to watch after the horse. Then, I walked the short distance to Crumbs and Casks. No one questioned the cloak I kept firmly in place and pulled low to cover my features.

It took some time before I spotted the boy, lurking in the shadows across the street. Not only was he a bully, he was also known for lifting coin from anyone too drunk to notice. Finishing my drink, I left the alehouse and walked down the street. When I was abreast with his shadow, I flicked a coin to him.

He caught it, his eyes wide with surprise.

"I have another one for you if you can answer a question for me."

"What's that?"

"Who was the boy with the cap today? The one with the king's insignia."

The boy snorted.

"Tommy Bell? That little shite is claiming he secretly

works for the king. No one believes him. You shouldn't neither."

"Where can I find Tommy Bell?"

The boy gave me directions to a home on the outskirts of town. I tossed him another coin even though he deserved a beating for his part in today's disturbance. He nodded his thanks and watched me shrewdly as I walked away. I wasn't a drunkard though, so I was safe.

After collecting the horse, I tried finding Tommy Bell's home on my own, but it was impossible to spot any landmarks or signs in the dark. Twice, men called out to me, and only my wits and a quick mare kept me safe.

Knowing I was running out of time, I turned back and made my way home, relieved to leave the late-night debauchery behind and annoyed I hadn't located the boy. My mind dwelled on how I would find my way back to town in the daylight. Hugh would never allow me to chase down some random boy. And, given Maeve's worry and understanding of my suspicions, I doubted she'd allow it either.

I was so lost in thought, I did not immediately notice the silence in the trees. The mare did. She snorted and sidestepped a moment before something launched itself at me from the trees. The mass collided with me and knocked me sideways off the horse. We landed with bruising force that numbed my arm and robbed me of breath.

While I lay stunned, my attacker ripped back my hood.

"You?" Kaven said.

I opened my mouth, not to speak but struggling to inhale.

His angry expression turned to worry as he rolled off of me and helped me sit up.

"Breath out first then in," he said.

I managed to regain my air on the second try.

"Are you hurt?" he asked.

Turning to him with an incredulous gaze, I punched him square in the nose.

"Of course I'm hurt, you ass! You knocked me off my damn horse!"

He pinched the bridge of his nose, sniffed, and blinked at me.

"You have no idea how grateful I am that you do not hit as hard as you knee."

"Please, allow me to try once more."

He stood and offered me his hand, standing at an angle lest I attempt to maim his manhood again.

I reached for the hand and stopped, realizing what I'd been about to do. Instead, I slapped his hand away.

"Is this how you lured them? Kindness? A trick?"

Hands now at his sides, he tilted his head to study me.

"Lured who?"

"I will not fall for your games," I said. I glanced at my horse, wondering if I could make it to her and mount before he caught me.

"Why are you out here, Eloise?"

"That's none of you concern."

"I believe it is."

"Well, I believe it's not. If you're not here to accost me or drag me into the trees to kill me, then I must be on my way." I stood cautiously, focused on him.

"That's a strange thing to say."

"Is it?" I said, arching a brow at him. "Our first meeting you threatened me. Our second meeting you physically accosted me, warranting the defense of my person. Both encounters were hardly shining examples of chivalry."

"Only those who threaten the Crown need fear me."

"That's hardly a comfort since you would be the one to determine what warrants a threat. Did picking berries on your land threaten the Crown? Does my presence here threaten the Crown?"

"Did you enter the king's retreat two days past?"

My pulse leapt, but I kept my fear from my expression.

"Why would I enter the king's retreat? That would be death, wouldn't it?"

He tucked his hands in his pockets and considered me.

"A simple trespassing would be a slap on the wrist. Maybe a public flogging. Stealing from the king would cost you far more than that. Did you take something?"

I snorted.

"Did you not hear me? I'm too smart to do something so stupid."

"Or perhaps you left something for the prince to find." He took a menacing step toward me.

"Touch me and I'll—"

"That's enough of that," he said, grabbing me and tossing me over his shoulder.

I kicked hard, connecting with the front of his thigh. He grunted and swatted me on the butt hard enough to elicit a squeal.

"You beastly pig ass son of a—"

"I'll do it again," he warned.

A moment later, I was sitting sideways on my horse with Kaven's hands on my thighs to steady me.

Our gazes locked as he looked up at me, and my breath caught. What was it about Kaven that made my good sense flee and my heart beat so erratically?

"You are by far the prickliest woman I have ever met. Are you dangerous, Eloise?" he asked, reigniting my ability to reason.

"Ask your testicles," I said.

With a swift nudge of my heel, I sent the mare flying, knocking Kaven aside in my haste to get away. His low chuckle followed me up the road.

My pulse didn't begin to slow until I reached the path to our house. I glanced over my shoulder before dismounting and continuing on foot. The road was empty as I'd guessed it would be. Unsure what that meant, I snuck into the barn and quietly unsaddled the mare. There wasn't much of a risk that Hugh would hear me and wake. Not with the tea that Anne used to make for Mother in his belly. Hugh, though, was the least of my worries.

"That was close," I said to the horse. "No more night

rides." She nickered softly as I wiped her down then returned her to her stall. With a quick check to ensure everything was in place, I left the stable.

All was silent as I let myself into the kitchen and tiptoed toward the dining room. There, I had to pause to wipe my palms on my dress. In my mind, I imagined Maeve hearing me and her expression of disappointment. Hadn't I vowed I wasn't like a child? Yet, here I was sneaking around like one.

Taking a calming breath, I made my way up the stairs without a creak. The candle still burned in our room, not an unusual sight.

When I slipped into the bedroom, I found Kellen sitting up in bed, a book open in her lap, just as I'd left her. Her gaze met mine, and I smiled slightly. She sighed, closed the book, and blew out the candle. In the dark, I got ready for bed.

However, even as I lay safe and comfortable in my own home, sleep escaped me.

My mind dwelled on my meeting with Kaven. The encounter had been all wrong. He'd aggressively knocked me from the horse, and I had been certain I'd found my end. Especially since I had bashed his head with a rock the last time we'd met. Yet, he'd offered his hand to help me to my feet, and everything after that had been wary and—I frowned—courteous. No, that smack on my backside had not been courteous. However, it had been earned. I grinned in the dark, remembering the punch to his nose and the kick.

My humor faded as I struggled to come up with an explanation for his behavior. Was Kaven even more dangerous than I thought? Did he seek to lull me? To what purpose, though?

CHAPTER TWELVE

"Must you be so loud?" I asked.

"Yes. It's not like you to sleep in. Wake up before it's noticed."

Sometimes, I hated Kellen's practical logic. I crawled out of bed and saw she'd already brushed out Judith's dress. Not a trace of dirt remained from my late-night encounter with Kaven.

"Thank you," I said.

She rolled her eyes at me and helped me with my hair as soon as my mourning dress was over my head. We'd just opened the door when Maeve stepped out of her room.

"Up late reading again?" she asked.

Kellen smiled.

"Mr. Bentwell's books are addicting. We will need another candle for our room, but I promise not to stay awake as long tonight."

Maeve waved away her concern.

"Reading is good for the mind."

Kellen's cheeks pinked as we made our way toward the stairs, and I blinked at my sister. There'd been only a handful of times I'd seen her flush.

She caught my look and shook her head slightly.

Keeping my question to myself, we followed Maeve to the entry where she stopped for her cloak.

"Promise that you'll stay inside while Hugh and I are gone," she said.

"I promise," Kellen and I said at the same time.

Maeve smiled.

"Good. Bar the doors until we return. Answer for no one." She hesitated. "I don't like leaving you like this."

"We will be fine," Kellen said. "If we hear something, we'll hide in the attic. No one will find us there."

Maeve nodded.

"We won't be long."

She opened the door and stepped out. The faint jangle of an approaching wagon stopped her from going further. She paused and looked back at us with a frown. I could see the indecision on her face.

"You've already turned away visitors and stated when we will receive guests. It won't look unusual for you to do the same today," Kellen said, moving to the door.

Maeve waved goodbye as Kellen closed it. She had her hand on the lock when she hesitated. She caught my look and shrugged.

"It would sound odd to our visitor if I slid the lock into place now."

I shook my head at her always considering mind.

"I'll go fix us breakfast. I'm hungry for hot oats this morning."

"That sounds lovely."

The door behind us opened before we reached the dining room. We both stopped and watched Maeve along with another woman enter.

"Fate saw fit to help us this morning," Maeve said, spotting us. "This is Sabine, Anne's cousin."

The young woman nodded to us.

"Anne's mother came to see me this morning. She said that Anne's taken a bit of leave and asked if I can step in for her to ensure she doesn't lose her position. I can cook and clean well, if you'll have me."

"We are very much in need of your assistance," Maeve said, "and we thank you for your kind offer."

"I'll fetch my bag from the wagon and tell my father that I'm staying."

Maeve waited until the girl left to look at us.

"I hope this is all right. I typically never hire without references."

"I'm sure this will be fine," Kellen said. "Better someone who knows Anne and won't be put out when she returns."

"Of course. And I'm so relieved I don't need to leave the two of you alone. I really must be off to speak with Mrs. Tiller. I feel terribly that she's already awake, thinking of her daughter," she waved at us again and hurried out the door, past Anne's cousin who was returning with her things.

Kellen discreetly bolted the door as soon as the woman was inside.

"Allow me to show you to your sleeping quarters and give you a tour of the kitchen," I said.

Less than an hour later, Kellen and I sat at the table eating the fruits of Sabine's labors.

"Is it all right?" she asked nervously.

"The best hot oats I've tasted," I assured her, taking another enthusiastic bite.

"I never knew toasting them could change the flavor so enjoyably," Kellen said.

The hot oats were truly good as was Sabine's company.

"I'm so grateful I could help. I was just released from the House of Cresstol." She sighed deeply. "My year was up. The mistress said she would give reference to any who asked, if Lady Grimmoire needs one."

"I think this is reference enough," I said, nodding toward my bowl.

"Do you think this position might be permanent once Anne returns?"

Kellen and I shared a subtle glance.

"It might be," Kellen said softly.

Sabine beamed.

"Mrs. Tiller had been vague about how long Anne would be gone, but I would happily fill in for Anne no matter the duration. Not that I'm hinting I want her position. I wouldn't do that to Anne."

"Of course not," Kellen agreed.

"Once you're finished, leave the dishes on the block. I'm going to go fetch some fresh linens for the beds."

She hurried from the room, already comfortable with our home's layout.

Kellen turned to me.

"Well? What happened last night? Do we know who's responsible?"

"I only know the boy's name. Tommy Bell. He lives on the southwest outskirts of town near a stable called the Whistling Steed."

"Sounds more like a name for an alehouse."

I flashed her a quick grin.

"I'd thought the same. Perhaps it would have been easier to find in the dark then. As it was, I had to give up and return home without speaking to our dear Tommy Bell. However, the boy who gave me his name said that Tommy claimed to be a secret messenger of the King but no one believed him."

"Not much of a secret if the boy is going around telling everyone."

"Very true. But that's not the oddest part of the evening," I said, carrying my bowl to the block.

"Oh?" she asked following me with hers.

"Kaven knocked me off my horse on my return home. I thought it would be the end of me."

"But it wasn't."

"No." I frowned and recalled our encounter. "After the initial fall, he seemed concerned, if still a little rude. He offered to help me up and called me prickly when I refused to believe he was actually kind. Then he plucked me off my feet and plopped me on my horse. I believe he truly intended to send me home mostly unscathed with only a few bruises."

Kellen's expression grew contemplative and distant as it often did when she needed to work something out. While she thought through the events, I led the way to the sitting room.

From above, I could hear the sound of Sabine's soft humming as she changed the linens. I hadn't realized how much I'd missed that simple normality.

"It makes no sense," Kellen said sitting in her chair. "Why knock you off the horse and then help you up? Why take Anne and Judith and not you?"

"My thoughts exactly. I can only suppose I was not the intended target. But why Mother and not us?"

She made a noncommittal sound and stared out the window.

"Even if you were not the intended target last night, if you were to ever be an intended target, why treat you cordially?"

Why indeed? Unless I never was the intended target. Or, perhaps, he wasn't the one to blame for Mother, Judith, and Anne. My heart stumbled at the possibility of his innocence then beat rapidly in hope.

"When I found Anne's cap by Mother's grave, I'd been so certain it was him that I damaged his testicles. Quite severely, given the sounds he made. That encounter alone makes his restraint in retribution last night even more curious."

"His testicles?" she said, looking at me with wide, disbelieving eyes.

"Don't look at me like that. He gave me no choice. It was his testicles or my life."

"Of course, I'm only surprised you still have your life. Doubly so now."

"Exactly my thoughts."

She absently picked up her book from the side table and opened it.

"This whole situation is nonsensical," she said. "Why take two maids and not you? Although we find value in Anne and Judith, you and I both know the majority of the world does not find value in those of lesser status. Even you and I only have as much value as where we live and whatever remains of Father's estate."

"Perhaps that's why I was let go," I said. "Perhaps there was an assumed value to my existence. Or, perhaps," I said, giving voice to what Kellen had said all along, "Kaven is not responsible for what has transpired. But if not him, then who?"

"As you've pointed out repeatedly, no one else makes

sense. All clues point back to Kaven. One kind act, which is out of character from all the other encounters, shouldn't so heavily sway us."

"You're right," I said. It was foolish to think his offered hand meant something more than a distraction.

"This will take some consideration," Kellen said.

"I agree. However, I hope it doesn't take us too long to determine his motivations. I worry for Sabine."

"The door is barred, and she's inside with us. For now, she's safe."

I sat in my chair and picked up my book as well. However, I struggled to read the words on the page. For, as much as I wanted to escape the reality of my circumstances, my mind continued to dwell on the problem of not only who killed my mother but how long it would be before someone else went missing?

THE SOUND of the entry door opening almost pulled my attention from the story. Although it had taken me a while to finally succumb to the melodic words of the author, I was now fully enraptured in the heroine's plight.

"Where are they?" I heard Maeve ask.

"In the sitting room, my lady."

The click of heels echoed in the hall, a note of agitation in the rhythm. It was that unusual sound that finally pulled me from the story and had me looking up. Kellen did the same.

Maeve entered looking weary and anxious.

"We had a bit of a delay leaving this morning. The horse had a stone lodged in its shoe. I must ask, did either of you take the horse last night?"

Kellen and I both wore twin expressions of surprise. Neither were faked.

"While I imagine that would be quite an adventure," Kellen said, "we both know it's not safe to venture out. Day or night. I much prefer my adventures to occur on the pages of my book. I fear my life is already too unpredictable for more."

"I quite agree," I said. "But it does bring to mind that I have been neglecting the animals. I haven't taken the pig for a walk in days." I closed my book. "I should probably correct that."

Maeve's gaze searched both of our faces. Her expression of upset faded to one of indulgence.

"You relieve me greatly," she said. "I don't know what I would do if one of you two disappeared in the middle of the night. If the pig needs a walk, it might be best to send Hugh."

I stood and walked to Maeve, taking her hand and giving it a light squeeze.

"It's not just the pig who needs a walk; I'm a bit restless with all of this time indoors. And, I don't mind walking him around the yard," I added quickly.

Any lingering doubt about us taking the horse last night seemed to vanish with my words.

"Of course. I'm sorry if I sounded accusing. Hugh swore he checked the mare before putting her up for the night."

I released her hand and hugged myself.

"He's not been himself with everything that's happening," I said, hating that I was diverting blame. "Perhaps he only overlooked it."

"I'm sure you're right. It's good that Sabine is here now. Is she settled in? I was so worried about the pair of you that I didn't ask."

"Yes, we gave her a tour of the house. However, I put off showing her the grounds. Now that you've returned, perhaps I could take her with me when I walk the pig."

"A splendid idea. While you do that, I think I might go lay down for a bit."

"Did it go poorly with Mrs. Tiller?" Kellen asked.

"The dear woman was quite surprised to see me this morning but very understanding when I explained what's been happening here and our request for her discretion. This whole ordeal is more taxing than I had imagined it would be."

Guilt nibbled at my conscience.

"We're sorry that we've burdened you," Kellen said.

"Nonsense. You're both a joy. It's everyone else who is the burden," she said with a conspiratorial smile. "I'll see you two at dinner."

She left the room, her steps slower than normal.

"I don't envy her that talk with Mrs. Tiller," I said softly.

"Neither do I. I'm guessing it didn't go as well as Maeve would like us to believe."

"I agree." I glanced at Kellen, who was vacantly gazing out the window once more. "Did you want to come outside with me?"

She shook her head. "My mind is busy. It's best I sit inside with my book."

I knew what she meant. She was still thinking over the problem of Kaven and his odd behavior. I knew that she, like me, was starting to doubt his guilt. But was it all just part of his ploy?

I went into the kitchen in search of Sabine and found her already preparing our evening meal.

"Would you like a tour of the yard?" I asked. "We have a few animals that I care for. The chickens are lovely for the fresh eggs. I usually put them there." I indicated the wooden bowl resting on the block. "We also have a pig that I'm caring for on behalf of someone else. He's not for eating."

Sabine smiled.

"That is a good thing because I don't know how to butcher a pig. However, I'm quite adept at pastries."

"I love pastries. There's a patch of—never mind. I can see you're busy." She wasn't that busy. However, I did not intend to tell her about the very berry patch where Judith disappeared.

Sabine wiped her hands on her apron.

"I'm never too busy to learn something new about the estate. I would love to accompany you. Let me just pull this off the fire so it doesn't scald."

She moved a simmering pot from the flames and grabbed her cloak.

Outside, I showed her the chickens first then the pig pen. The pig wasn't rooting about, which I found odd. And I realized I hadn't fed him yet that morning.

"Pig," I called, opening the gate. "It's time for a walk."

I heard a shuffling sound from the shelter at the back of the pen. Taking care where I stepped and lifting my skirts to avoid the muck, I approached his dwelling.

"Come now, pig. You know you must walk."

When I ducked down to peer in, an ear-splitting squeal rent the air at the same time the pig came flying at me. I just barely straightened in time to avoid being trampled. The large creature darted for the gate at full speed. I didn't know what he intended, since I'd closed it behind me. He seemed to notice it was closed at the last moment and came to a thunderous stop.

His sides heaved as he spun around looking for another avenue of escape.

"Miss Eloise, perhaps you should climb the fence," Sabine called.

I didn't move, keeping my attention on the pig. I'd never seen him act so crazed before.

"Are you hurt, Mr. Pig?" I asked softly. "Do you need

tending?" I held out my hand. "You know I won't hurt you. Come now. Let's have a look at you."

The pig shook his ears and let out a series of squeals and grunts before trotting toward me. While I did my best to remain outwardly calm, I prepared myself to scramble over the fence if the pig decided it no longer wanted to be docile.

Slowing a few feet from me, the pig bumped his head against my hand.

"There now," I said softly, looking him over and seeing nothing amiss. "Did I startle you out of a nap?"

The pig seemed to calm, and I walked over to the sheltered rack where I kept his tether.

"Should we walk?" I asked.

The pig grunted and seemed his normal self once again.

"He normally doesn't act like that," I said, trying to assure Sabine who watched the pig with doubt. "He's quite tame and enjoys his walks. Usually I take him in the woods, but for today, we'll keep him to the yard."

"That's a sound idea. I think it would be best if I returned to the kitchen." I didn't try to stop her retreat. Pigs weren't for everyone.

My portly companion and I walked around the yard once then down the driveway. I would have turned there to come back, but the pig caught the scent of something and started up the road toward the retreat. He didn't go far before veering off the path to a thicket of bramble on the side.

"You have a knack for intruding," a voice said.

I jumped and the pig squealed, almost jarring my arm from its socket before he tore his tether out of my grasp. Thankfully the pig didn't go far, only just behind me as if using me as a shield. I looked from the pig to Kaven.

"It looks like you startled your brother," I said to the man.

Kaven snorted.

"Even the sounds you make are similar," I added.

"A bee's sting is much kinder than your sharp words," Kaven replied with a scowl.

I shrugged.

"If you don't like my reaction, perhaps you should stop jumping out at me."

"Fair enough. I was hoping I would see you today." There was something in his tone—Menace? Annoyance?— that had me retreating a step.

"I think I need to return," I said.

"Stay." The command was followed by a sudden hand around my arm.

I stared up at Kaven, wondering how he'd gotten so close so fast. With barely a thought, I fisted my hand to strike out. He caught my intended jab with ease, his fingers closing over my own.

"I have never met a woman as violent as you. Was your mother like this?"

"Do not speak of my mother," I hissed before trying to stomp on his foot.

He deftly moved out of my way.

"I'm learning your tricks," he said with a smirk. "What will you do now, my little wasp? You've nothing left but words."

"Pig," I said, "if ever you were to repay my care of you, now would be the time."

"Are you speaking to—"

Both of our eyes widened as the pig let out a crazed squeal and knocked into me. I flew into Kaven, sending us both to the ground. Kaven grunted at the double impact of his back hitting the ground and me landing on top of him.

I scrambled off of him with all haste, accidentally clipping his manhood this time.

"Sorry," I said even as I scooped up the pig's tether and sprinted for the house.

The pig kept up with me every step of the way. When we reached the pen, I scratched his ear.

"You're a very fine friend," I said. "Thank you."

The pig grunted as I closed the pen, and I pretended not to notice the way his too human gaze followed me.

CHAPTER THIRTEEN

KELLEN WAS MISSING FROM THE SITTING ROOM WHEN I returned. Rather than seek her out, I went to the kitchen to check on Sabine. I spent the rest of the day listening to idle stories about Sabine's prior employers and the life of gentry in general. Hearing their common disregard for those they employed helped ease some of my guilt that Sabine was staying with us. Surely, with Kellen and I both watching her, she would be safe.

When dinner was ready, I went to wake Maeve. It felt odd to knock softly on her door and hear a voice other than Mother's.

"I'm sorry to wake you," I said through the panel. "Dinner is ready."

"I'll be right there," Maeve called. "Thank you for waking me."

Leaving her door, I checked our room for Kellen. Her book was lying open on her bed but Kellen was absent. Panic squeezed my chest. I whirled to tell Maeve and almost ran into my sister.

"Curse you, Kellen," I said irritably for the twofold scare she'd given me.

Her lips twitched.

"Were you looking for me?"

"You know I was. Dinner is ready."

"So I heard."

I moved toward the stairs, my annoyance clinging to me. Kellen reached out and clasped my hand.

"It wasn't intentional. This time," she said.

Her lingering humor and honest admission broke through my irritation.

"I hope someday you meet someone as in love with tricks as you are. Then you'll understand how unpleasant they can be."

"If they're so unpleasant, why do you always laugh?"

I grinned and shook my head. I never could stay mad at Kellen for long.

"Where were you?" I asked.

"In the attic."

"Did you finish your book already?" I asked as we reached the bottom step.

A scrape of noise above us had me turning to smile at Maeve.

"If you've finished, we can go to town tomorrow to fetch more," Maeve said.

"I haven't finished. It only reached a part that didn't sit well with me, so the book and I needed to part company for a while."

I chuckled.

In the dining room, Sabine had the table set and waiting. She lifted the cover from a bowl to reveal a light spring soup and removed a towel sheltering a basket of fluffy biscuits.

"These look delightful," I said, reaching for one.

Maeve complimented Sabine's skills after the first bite. I could tell the young woman desperately wanted to please us so she could secure a place for herself. While I liked her, I hoped her position wouldn't be as Judith or Anne's replacement. I wanted our friends safely returned. Yet, with each passing day, my hope of that happening was dwindling.

After dinner, Maeve and Sabine went to the sitting room to discuss supplies and expenses. Kellen grabbed me by the hand and dragged me upstairs. Instead of taking us to our bedroom as I expected, she led me to the attic.

When I'd last been up there, the space had been a disorganized mess of oil-cloth covered furniture. Since then, pieces had been moved and recovered, creating little pockets of space.

Kellen noticed my surprise at the change.

"Maeve had mentioned a delay in the arrival of her possessions, and I wanted to be sure there was enough storage space for anything that did not fit downstairs."

"How can you spend so much time up here?" I asked, suppressing a shiver and wishing for my cloak.

She just smiled as she guided me toward the back of the room. Finally, she stopped at a large stack of furniture and lifted one of the oil-cloths to reveal a small crawl space.

"After you," she said, motioning. "And keep quiet."

I crawled through a short tunnel and emerged into a cleared space within the cluster of furniture. A swath of oil-cloth created a ceiling for the nook. Moving further in, I sat on the floor and looked at the exposed items. There were books and an oil lamp and a chest.

Kellen came in behind me and noticed my shiver.

"It will warm well enough with both of us in here." She went to the chest and lifted the lid. "Mother saved strands of our hair, clothing, and other things in here," she said. "This is where I found the letters. They were at the very bottom. I thought they were nothing more than memories of the past, like the rest of the items. Then, I found this."

She reached toward the lid and pulled back a few inches of the fabric that lined the inside. Underneath, was a bit of parchment.

She removed and unfolded it. I leaned close to read it with her.

. . .

Margaret,

Although my heart is heavy, I have not forgotten my promise. For the remainder of your life and that of your children, I grant you and your family use of the caretaker's cottage for the royal retreat north of Towdown. The retreat was Sevil's favorite place to visit, and I cannot see myself going there without her.

For all that you've done and sacrificed for the good of this kingdom and my family, I pledge my aid should you and your family ever have need.

Be well in life, Margaret. When we meet again, I hope it is in a safer time with far better circumstances.

Aftan, King of Drisdall

I looked up at Kellen, stunned.

"I do not know what Mother did," she said, "but given the contents of this letter, I cannot believe her death is the result of the Crown."

My initial surprise gave way to a slow, burning anger.

"That means whoever killed her is acting against the Crown. And this letter gives us the audience we would need to present our case."

"Once we have proof," Kellen said.

"Yes. Once we have proof. I need to speak with Tommy Bell."

"I agree. However, there seems to be a second mystery surrounding this house," Kellen said, folding the letter.

"What do you mean?"

"There were three other letters with this one," she said. "Not from the King, but from Elspeth."

I frowned recalling what my sister had said about the letters she'd read thus far.

"Mother hid away three letters from her but not the rest?"

"Precisely why they intrigue me."

She handed over the letters.

I HOPE *this letter finds you in good health, dear one. The ban on magic is making my search more difficult than I anticipated. However, I am certain I grow closer each day to discovering the identity of the one who killed the Queen. Keep the babes safely hidden until I can return.*

E

I LOOKED UP AT KELLEN.

"Hidden?"

"Keep reading."

. . .

I'm relieved to hear that the children are thriving despite the situation of their births. It is something that has weighed on my mind greatly since I left you. My search is not progressing as I had hoped. Every location spell I cast returns nothing. There is another spell I might try. However, we both know the cost of that which is cast in blood.

Keep the babes safely hidden until I can return.

E

I quickly read the last one.

Time is passing too quickly. I fear I may need to give up this search or face too many questions when I finally settle somewhere. Kiss the babes for me and tell them that I will come to collect my charge from you soon.

E

I looked up at Kellen.

"Mother knew a caster," I said in awe.

"Very well, it would seem, if she had planned to give one of us over to the woman."

I frowned and read the last letter again but could not refute Kellen's suspicion.

"So it would seem. I wonder what happened."

"Perhaps whatever spell she thought to cast had a deadly result as she hinted it might."

"Or she was caught casting and sent to the forest," I said.

I placed the letters on the floor and studied them.

"You're right that there's a second mystery. What did Mother do for the kingdom that would warrant a letter of protection from the king? And why would she give one of us to a caster, the very type of person who was outlawed by the king?" I exhaled, trying not to let my frustration gain control of me. "Do you think Maeve would know anything about the events surrounding our births? The second letter alludes to something."

"Doubtful. Mother never mentioned her cousin. If Maeve was present at our births, I would think she would have been included in whatever events Mother had been involved in and would have remained in our lives. Despite that, I did consider approaching Maeve with this, but you saw her today. She's exhausted and has enough to worry over."

"Where does that leave us?"

"In the same ignorant position we were previously. That hasn't changed. The letter only proves the King thought of Mother in a kind light at one time. We know too little to assume more than that. You need to speak with Tommy Bell."

Hearing that statement, I knew she was officially

releasing me from my promise to forget what was happening around us.

"You believe things will get worse, don't you?" I asked.

"I do."

Trying to dispel the chill her answer had given me, I looked around the space again.

"Was it like this when you found it?" I asked.

"It was." She returned the letters to their hiding place. "I think Mother used to come up here, too."

She'd come up here and hidden the letters she had received from Elspeth and the King. She'd also hidden the truth from us.

"Why didn't she tell us any of this?" I wondered.

"I don't know, but I doubt that knowing the tale behind those letters will change the course of events before us."

"I'll try again tonight," I said.

"Tonight? You were lucky last time. We should wait until tomorrow and find a reason to go to town."

"You know Maeve will not permit us out of Hugh's sight long enough to track down this boy. And, I'm less concerned about the dark than I am about letting these disappearances continue without hindrance. I will be safe tonight as I was last night."

Kellen gave me a doubtful look but didn't argue.

"Look at this," she said instead. She plucked one of the books from its position on the floor and handed it to me. I opened the cover and skimmed the hand-written scrawl that described the medicinal purposes of several plants.

"At first glance, these books seem like simple herbalist notes. However, I've been reading them and have come across other things. Potions."

I looked up from the book.

"These are books on magic?"

"I have a lot more reading to do before I can say that, but I believe so."

"Why would Mother keep books of magic?"

"I don't believe they were Mother's. Elspeth was a caster by her own admission. Based on her letters, she intended to return here."

"I'm glad she didn't." I couldn't imagine a life without Kellen beside me.

After crawling out of the hidden nook, Kellen showed me around the rest of the attic. There were many pieces that I could now see had never belonged to my parents. Having read the king's letter, I understood from where much of the furniture had come.

We returned to our room and settled in for an evening of reading while we waited for Maeve to retire. However, the candle burned low without a sound from below.

Kellen and I went to check on Maeve's whereabouts and found her in the sitting room still at the desk. She seemed lost in thought until we entered. She looked up at us with clear eyes and a smile.

"Is everything all right, dears?"

"Yes," Kellen said. "We were worried since you hadn't come upstairs yet and wanted to check on you."

"You're so sweet. I seem to have an abundance of energy from my nap and much too much to think on. I cannot seem to find the deed for this house. It shouldn't pose any problems, but it is a curiosity given its proximity to the king's retreat. I don't suppose you know how your parents came to own such a property."

"Actually, I was rather hoping that would be a story you could share with us," I said. "Mother and Father never mentioned it, and we never thought to ask."

Maeve sighed.

"I thought as much. I'm sure we will find the deed somewhere. I'll check the papers in your father's room tomorrow. Meanwhile, I'll keep going over the books. Don't stay up too late tonight. Growing girls need their rest."

She looked at the papers, and I knew she was already distracted with whatever she had found there.

Kellen and I quietly withdrew, leaving Maeve to her thoughts. Back in our room with the door closed, Kellen tried to dissuade me from leaving that night.

"She has to sleep eventually," I said softly.

"Until she does, you had better change into your bedclothes. It would look suspicious if you're fully dressed if she comes to check on us."

Kellen's forethought saved us from being caught as Maeve did indeed check on us hours later.

"Still up reading?" she asked when she poked her head in. "I picked up one of your books, Kellen, and can understand what holds your attention so thoroughly."

Kellen blushed.

"They are quite difficult to put down," I agreed, wondering why my sister was acting so oddly.

"Can I fetch either of you something from the kitchen? I found some ledgers that detail your father's accounts, and fear I'll be up with them all night."

"We're fine, thank you," Kellen said.

I smiled and agreed.

As soon as Maeve closed the door, Kellen and I blew out the candle by silent agreement. There was no point in staying up that night.

We woke late the next morning to grey skies and a light rain, and I knew there would be no sneaking off that day either. The delay festered in my mind as an ominous sign. The need to do something crawled over my skin like an army of ants. It took every ounce of restraint to calmly lounge in the sitting room with a book in my lap all morning.

When a carriage rattled up the drive after our midday meal, Kellen and I hid in the kitchen with Sabine.

"Do you get visitors often?" she asked.

"Often enough," I said. "It seems that the Prince is returning and will be in residence at the retreat soon. It has many of the townspeople curious. They come here under the pretense of condolences and the false belief that we know more than they."

"I heard much the same news about the Prince while still at the House of Cresstol," Sabine said. "No one seems to know when he'll arrive, though. Everyone is waiting for banners to go up at the castle. A sure sign of an imminent welcome."

"Do you miss town life?" Kellen asked.

"No, miss. I quite like the quiet here. You two and Lady Grimmoire are gracious and kind. Not everyone in town can boast those traits."

She had shared enough stories that I believed her.

"Sometimes the quiet can be a bit dull," Kellen said.

I turned to give her a disbelieving look, and she kicked me under the table. With relief, I kicked her back, glad that she was up to something rather than calling our mother's death and the subsequent disappearances of our friends dull.

"I can imagine it might seem that way to two young girls. Maeve is sending me to town tomorrow with Hugh for some supplies. Would you like to accompany us?"

"That would be lovely," I said, appreciating my sister's wit.

"PLEASE STAY OUT OF TROUBLE," Maeve said before she waved then went inside.

"Do you two cause trouble often?" Sabine asked from her place on the seat beside Hugh.

"Rarely," Kellen said. "However, trouble does have a way of finding us."

I elbowed her.

"That was before Maeve spoke with the families of the boys who were causing us trouble. Since then, we've been trouble free."

"True," Kellen agreed.

We both glanced at Hugh, who had remained impassive through the whole conversation. He hit a particularly large divot in the road that lifted Kellen and me from our places in the back. She landed with a wince.

"I miss the carriage already," she said under her breath.

"Your backside has grown too soft," I said with a smirk, hiding my own wince. I would have preferred the carriage as well; however, the need for supplies necessitated the wagon.

The jostling ride had thoroughly bruised my backside by the time we reached town. Kellen watched me with a knowing grin as I eased from the wagon.

"Shall we meet here again in three hours?" Sabine asked.

"Meet?" Hugh said. "We should stay together."

Sabine laughed.

"I believe the last thing these two want is to stay with us while we're purchasing boring supplies."

"I did finish my book last night," Kellen said, lifting the bag at her side which did indeed hold a book. We'd come prepared with a reason to go off on our own. We hadn't anticipated Sabine proposing we do so.

"They'll be fine," Sabine said. "This isn't their first trip to town. If you two run into any trouble, I'm sure you'll find us easily enough in the market."

I nodded in agreement and hooked my arm through Kellen's.

"We might even read a book while we're there," she said. "I do like those slim volumes Mr. Bentwell has on the shelf by his desk."

As she spoke, I turned us toward the book shop, and we started on our way. When Hugh didn't stop us, I knew we'd won our way free of his company.

Turning the corner, Kellen and I stopped.

"Should we stay together, or should one of us go to Mr. Bentwell's?" she asked.

"I think it would look more suspicious if we split up."

"Together then."

It took us over an hour to walk to the outskirts of town and navigate the landmarks the boy had given me. Our dresses, even though mourning black, were too fine for the area. However, no one gave us more than a single curious glance as we passed.

I found the Bell home and knocked on the door. By luck, the young man in question answered.

"Are you Tommy Bell?" I asked politely.

He gave me a suspicious look, but there was no recognition in his eyes at the sight of Kellen or me.

"What if I were? What would you want with me?"

Kellen produced a copper to show him.

"We have a few harmless questions to ask you," she said.

He snatched the coin.

"What do ya want to know?"

"First, can you show me the king's cap you're said to have? It will prove that we are indeed speaking with Tommy Bell," I said.

"Just a moment," he said before he dashed off inside and returned with the cap in question sitting atop his head.

"You look quite dapper in that," Kellen said.

"What's dapper mean?"

"You look well-dressed and handsome," I clarified.

He grinned.

"Can you tell me how you came by such a hat?" Kellen asked.

"It's a king's hat. How do you think I came by it?"

"I'm afraid I have no idea how one comes to be in the service of the king, but I'm desperate to try to be a messenger myself," I said.

Kellen produced another coin.

"We promise not to accept any message from the king unless you've had a chance to take it first."

He studied us for a long moment.

"I wish I could help you. I truly do. I don't exactly recall how I came by this hat."

"What do you mean?" I asked.

"Well, I remember standing in the dark, watching for any

abandoned dregs. My da likes when I can bring something home for him. A man came up to me and asked me a question. It was dark, and I couldn't see him clearly. Dark hair. Tall." He shrugged. "He gave me a package and told me to deliver it. Then he gave me the cap and a coin to see the job done."

"Where did this chap send you?"

"I don't know," he said.

As he answered, a flash of unnatural green light reflected in his eyes.

CHAPTER FOURTEEN

I STARED AT YOUNG TOMMY BELL UNTIL THE LIGHT FADED. Without a doubt, it was the same light I'd seen in my mother's eyes before she died. However, Tommy remained whole and healthy, if increasingly more uncomfortable the longer I stared.

"Thank you, Tommy," Kellen said, taking my arm. "We'll try hanging around the alehouses and hope for the best. Have a pleasant day."

I nodded and managed a smile before Kellen led us away.

"You saw it too, didn't you?" I asked.

"I did."

"What do you think it means?" I asked.

"That we're even further from the truth than before. Why would a king, who put a ban on the use of magic, use magic to influence a young lad to deliver a package? Had it been from the King, his guard would have only needed to ask the boy, and young Tommy would have excitedly done it for the cap alone."

"Kaven is acting on his own."

"He has dark hair then? Kaven?"

I'd forgotten that Kellen had never had the displeasure of meeting him.

"In the light it's a warm brown. Darker than my hair, but far lighter than yours. At night..." I shrugged. "I suppose it could be dark if one weren't paying much attention."

She glanced knowingly at me. I'd been paying far too much attention to mistake his hair as dark.

"Then, I believe Kaven is acting without the king's knowledge. However, Kaven is the prince's servant. Perhaps this is a son's act against his father?"

I growled in frustration.

"I'm done with this game and want it over."

"And how do you propose ending it?"

"We know the king isn't involved, and we have the letter promising help. I say we confront Kaven to discover the truth and go to the king with whatever admission Kaven makes."

"And if there is no admission?"

I stopped walking and glared at Kellen.

"Are you being difficult for a reason?"

"Yes. To spare us both additional misery. If someone is willing to use magic and take people while daylight is shining, do you honestly believe they will openly admit their transgression? If Kaven is the culprit, you'll find yourself taken like Judith and Anne. And, I'll find myself without a sister. If Kaven isn't the culprit, you'll survive the encounter but likely cause a stir which is exactly what Maeve is working so hard to avoid."

Defeated by her logic, I started walking again.

"Then what would you have us do?"

"For now, I would have us arriving at Mr. Bentwell's post-haste."

Thanks to Kellen's ever-present cache of coins, we hired a small carriage to deliver us to the bookshop in mere minutes. We returned the read books and selected new ones at our leisure before returning to the market. We'd only just rounded the corner when we spotted Hugh and Sabine.

I waved and smiled.

"I hope you had enough time," Sabine said. "I hadn't anticipated Hugh's speed when I suggested three hours."

"It was plenty of time to select new books," Kellen said.

The ride home was quiet and much more comfortable, thanks to the bags of flour, sugar, and dried beans that Kellen and I used as seats.

When we arrived home, there was already a carriage in the drive.

"Bollocks, I'd best get inside. I'd hoped we'd left early enough that I would be back to answer the door for any guests."

"It's nothing to worry over," Kellen said. "Maeve doesn't mind answering it."

Sabine gave a grateful smile and hurried inside.

"Do you need any help carrying the supplies in?" I asked Hugh.

"No."

I hated that he was still hurting so.

"All right then. I think I'll take the pig for a walk before I go inside to read."

Kellen shot me a warning look.

"I know to stay on our property," I said. "I'm quite capable of listening, and Hugh will be in the yard if I need to call for help."

Neither tried to stop me as I went for the pig's tether. More than anything, I just needed time to think. I knew that Kellen had no idea what to do next. I didn't either. And that was entirely unacceptable.

Taking the pig, who was much more docile today, I started toward Mother's clearing.

"Stay close," Hugh warned.

I waved to acknowledge that I heard him and disappeared into the woods, not taking the path but veering to the left toward the ridge to make a slow circle of our property and avoid going anywhere near the retreat. The pig stopped occasionally to root in bracken and produced a few truffles.

Holding the black misshapen globes, I recalled the old woman at the Brazen Belle.

DEFIANT

"Mr. Pig, these truffles are lovely, but the old woman who gave you to me said you can do better. She also said I should cut your portions even further."

The pig's head jerked up from where he'd been rooting, and he let out a concerned squeal.

I sighed.

"I wish my life was as simple as worrying over whether or not I would have enough to eat. What am I to do, Mr. Pig? Why are my friends disappearing? I would give anything to know where they are."

The pig grew agitated, pacing in a circle and grunting and squealing.

"Hush, my friend. I won't cut your portions. I intend to walk you more. I'll help you become the trim handsome pig I know you to be."

He stopped squealing and looked at me. Again, I was struck by how human some of his responses seemed. He probably just knew food and work-related words like "portion" and "walk."

"Come on," I said. "Let's keep walking."

He huffed a great breath then started trotting along the ridge, his nose to the ground. I didn't often walk him this way for fear that the land would give way under his weight and we would go tumbling to the trees below.

Near the pines tucked a fair distance from the back of the shed, the pig stopped abruptly. He grunted softly several times. However, he didn't otherwise move, his gaze fixated on the cluster of pines still a length away.

The absence of the birdsong, or any other noise beyond my breathing, created an unnatural hush as if the forest was waiting for what might happen next. It unnerved me as did the pig's odd behavior.

"What is it?" I asked the pig.

He walked around me and nudged me forward. I took two halting steps toward the evergreens, my skin prickling with trepidation.

"Perhaps we should—" The pig jostled me from behind, sending me into the dense green branches. He gave several squeals and grunts when I turned to look back at him. Human fear shown in his intelligent eyes, but he still moved toward me as if to continue nudging me along.

"I'm going," I said. "Don't hurry me."

He quieted and waited. Facing the trees, I took a step back to try to peer through the dense branches.

"Is anyone here?" I whispered.

Not a sound came from inside. Yet the tingle of awareness, of not being alone, continued. My hands shook as I pushed against the needled branches that caught in my hair and tugged at my clothes. Closing my eyes against the onslaught, I continued forward until I suddenly broke free.

My foot caught on something, and I went tumbling forward, a thick layer of needles cushioning my fall. Rolling to my side, I looked back at what had caused my fall.

Near the base of the trees lay two bodies. Skin wrinkled and shriveled like old grapes, they could have been there any number of years. Yet, the dresses and hair told me otherwise.

I'd found Anne and Judith.

My chest tightened, and my eyes watered as I stared at the remains of the two people I held dear. Their mouths were open and their hands partially raised as if to stave off an attack. What horrors had they faced before their deaths?

A questioning grunt drew me from my grief. I wiped my eyes and got to my feet, pushing my way through the branches once more. I fell to my knees before the pig.

"How did you know?" I asked, voice breaking.

He grunted and snuffled my hair. I let myself believe he was consoling me. I needed it.

"What am I to do?"

Although it was quite obvious the pair had died because of magic, I remained no closer to discovering who had killed them. The only clues I had were based on the conversation from young Tommy Bell. A man with dark hair.

However, Kellen was right that we couldn't assume it was Kaven, alone. Only one thing remained certain. We still had no idea who or what we were dealing with.

Getting to my feet, I started toward the house. I barely noticed the pig following me until it bumped my legs when we passed his pen. I opened the gate and watched the pig trot in. He went straight for his little shelter and hid away inside. I wished I could hide away somewhere, too.

With heavy steps, I went to the house. Poor Mr. and Mrs. Tiller. Anne was their only child. From Anne, I knew they had hopes she would remarry someday. Now, that would never happen.

Judith was, no, Judith had been Mother's age. Content with her spinster status, she'd happily worked for our family. Her own Mother and Father were being cared for by her siblings in a small village north of here. She hadn't gone home often, but I knew she'd still be missed by her loved ones. By us.

The kitchen door opened despite my numbed fingers. I hadn't even realized I'd gotten so cold.

"Eloise?" Kellen said, setting her book on the table and coming to me. "What's wrong?"

Sabine, who was at the cutting board, stopped her meal prep to come toward us. I looked at them both, feeling the tears gather again.

"I found Judith and Anne. Their bodies were left in a cluster of trees behind the shed."

Sabine covered her mouth with her hand, her eyes wide. Kellen took me by the arm and led me to the stool near the fire. As soon as I was seated, she moved away from me.

"Can you discreetly request Maeve's presence, Sabine?" she asked.

I looked at the pale woman and doubted any interruption would be subtle, given her state. Kellen seemed to think the same thing.

"Never mind. I'll fetch Maeve. Can you make some tea for Eloise?"

Sabine nodded, and Kellen left us in the kitchen. The silence grew deafening.

"I thought Anne was away visiting someone," she finally said.

"Anne disappeared in the middle of the day several days ago. Judith disappeared a few days before that. When Judith disappeared, we'd hoped she'd gone to visit her family. But, we checked, and they hadn't heard from her. When Anne disappeared, we reported the disappearances to the guard. They were unbothered by two housemaids gone missing."

Sabine joined me near the fire, slowly sitting on the other stool there.

"Could you tell what got them? Was it a wolf?" She shivered lightly. "I heard tales of a sickness and death years ago because of creatures from the Dark Forest."

"It was no creature from the forest," I said. "It was magic."

The door opened just as I spoke those last words. Maeve walked in with concern on her face.

"Eloise, we talked about you casting these accusations. Sabine, you mustn't listen to her."

"They're dead," I said. "Judith and Anne. I found their bodies between the ridge and the shed. It looks like the life was drawn from them, leaving behind nothing but dried husks. Without their clothes or their hair, they would have been unrecognizable."

Maeve stared at me as if weighing the truth of my words.

I stood.

"Come. I will show you."

"That's not necessary, Eloise. You're shaking. First, let's fix you some tea to calm your nerves."

I shook my head.

"The shaking will likely continue no matter what I drink. They're out there. Alone. Abandoned. Dead."

Sabine took my hand.

"Not abandoned," she said. "We will fetch them and bury them."

Maeve said nothing more as I led the way out the door. Hugh emerged from the shed when we neared.

"You had better come with us," Maeve said quietly. "We will need your strength."

No one spoke as I followed the path back to the trees and pushed my way into the hidden clearing. Sabine started crying when she saw what was left of her cousin. Kellen and Maeve paled but neither shed a tear. Maeve didn't know them well enough, and Kellen would never let herself feel that deeply. It didn't matter. I cried enough for both of them.

"There's room next to Mother," Kellen said. "Judith and Anne would like it there."

Sabine shook her head.

"It is a kind offer, but Anne belongs with her parents. And I'm sure Judith's kin would want her close as well."

"You're right," Maeve said. She took a calming breath. "Hugh and I will wrap the bodies and place them in the wagon. It's getting too late to travel to town tonight." I hadn't even noticed the darkening sky. "It would be safer to leave at first light."

Sabine looked at the bodies and quickly agreed.

"Back inside, girls. A calming tea will help you sleep tonight."

"Lady Grimmoire, thank you for the offer to care for the bodies, but such work is better left to me. I'll help Hugh then finish dinner."

"Don't worry about dinner," Kellen said. "Eloise and I will finish it."

"Very well," Maeve said. She stepped toward Sabine and hugged her. "I'm so sorry for the misfortune that has befallen your family."

Sabine hugged her in return. "Thank you, My Lady."

Kellen and I followed Maeve back to the house. While we cooked, Maeve paced in the kitchen.

"Do you still believe this to be the work of the King?" she asked, stopping abruptly.

"I'm not certain," I said. "There are many reasons to believe these deaths are related to the Royal Family. The arrival of the prince's servants the day of Mother's death. The King's insignia on the messenger's hat. And there is very little evidence to direct the blame elsewhere."

Maeve took my hands in her own.

"You must stop saying such things."

"What should we say?"

"Nothing."

I couldn't stop my look of disbelief.

"I understand your anguish and need for justice. But if you accuse the Crown of killing by use of magic with or without proof, you'll die, and your sister will truly be alone."

I glanced at Kellen who continued to cook as she listened to our exchange. Maeve's concern was very real and exactly Kellen's fear. Yet, it was the risk that something might happen to Kellen that spurred my insistence.

"And if the next victim is Kellen? What good will my silence have done?"

Maeve released my hands and considered me for a quiet moment.

"Kellen? Would you mind terribly if I spoke with Eloise privately?"

Kellen and I shared a look. We didn't keep secrets.

"Of course," Kellen said.

"Come with me, Eloise." Maeve turned and left the room. I quickly followed.

She led the way upstairs to her room. It was still empty save for the small bed in the side room and the large bag of clothes which she'd arrived with. She went to the bag and withdrew a folded piece of paper.

"I had hoped to never share this with you," she said.

"You and Kellen have been through so much. But I need you to understand everything." She clasped my hand once more. "You and Kellen mean much to me. I want to keep you safe. To protect you from everything that is happening. It was what your father wished, too." She released my hand and looked down at the folded paper.

"Tell me honestly, Eloise...do you really think your father went to the Dark Forest to find a trade route?"

"Yes," I said firmly.

Maeve smiled sadly.

"I disagree. He loved your mother very much. Losing her hurt him in ways we will never understand."

I felt sick at what she was saying. Yes, my father had loved my mother very much, but so much that he had given up on life?

"I don't believe that."

"I know." She handed over the piece of paper.

I unfolded it and stared at the official document. A marriage license. Father's signature was on it along with Lady Grimmoire's.

"This is why I don't think he will return. The moment he heard of your mother's death, we wed. There is no love between us. He meant to leave you with someone who could protect you in full until you were ready to start your own lives."

The enormity of my situation hit me hard, and my hands started to tremble. Father wasn't coming back.

Mother was gone. Judith and Anne were dead. All that remained in my world was Kellen.

"Why are you showing me this now?"

"You'd just lost your mother, and I didn't have the heart to tell you that you'd lost your father as well. I thought I could spare you. Discovering these deaths has changed that. Now, I worry that I won't be able to protect you. Especially if you choose to pursue the accusation of the Crown in the death of your mother, Judith, and Anne. I hope showing you this will help you understand why I'm urging you against it. Kellen needs you right now. She follows your lead while holding herself apart from all others. You are her strength. What would she do without you?"

"How will remaining idle keep us safe?" I asked.

"We won't remain idle. I will go to town and hire more help. More men like Hugh to protect the grounds. And you and Kellen will stay out of the woods."

I bowed my head and studied the document. How could everything have changed so much in that single moment of placing the necklace on Mother?

"I will not pursue my accusation of the Crown," I said looking up. "Unless there is no other choice. We will hide in the house, for now."

Maeve hugged me, her relief visible.

"Thank you, Eloise. And forgive me for telling you as I did." She pulled back to look at me. "I think it would be best not to tell Kellen of this. I fear for her wellbeing. She grieves so deeply already, keeping her pain to herself. Knowing that your father most likely will not return..."

I nodded and handed the license back.

Shortly after we returned to the kitchen, Sabine entered. Her silent, tear-streaked face reminded me that Kellen and I were not alone in our grief.

"I'm sorry for your loss," I said.

Sabine gave me a half-hearted smile as she sat on the stool by the fire and accepted a cup of the tea that Kellen had brewed.

"Thank you. And I am sorry for yours. I will leave with Anne and Judith at first light. There is no doubt now that magic was involved. We may not know who is to blame, but certainly the guard will have to give credence to the issue of their disappearance once they see the remains."

"I agree," said Maeve. "Judith and Anne serve as irrefutable proof that something is amiss in these woods."

CHAPTER FIFTEEN

THE MOMENT THE COCK'S CROW SOUNDED, I FLEW OUT OF bed. I'd meant to wake before first light, but Kellen and I had stayed up late talking. Despite Maeve's warning to keep the news of her marriage to Father a secret, I had told Kellen. She had a right to know even if the information hurt her.

"Kellen, wake up." I hurried to slip into my dress as my sister sat up. "We're going to miss saying goodbye to Sabine."

That sparked some life into Kellen. She got out of bed and washed her face, the slight puffiness around her eyes barely noticeable. It hurt to know that she'd cried because of Father's abandonment of us. But it made me more determined to speak to Sabine again about bringing the bodies to the guard. If she was able to convince the guard that something was happening here on the king's lands, help would come quickly. And, perhaps we could then petition the king for help finding our father.

"What if they accuse her?" Kellen asked softly.

"Sabine wasn't hired on until after Mother, Judith, and Anne had already died. It would make no sense to accuse her."

"Very little in this world ever makes sense."

I gave her a quick hug.

"One look at those bodies, and the King's guards will know magic is involved. They'll come help. The forest will be full of them, and they won't rest until they find the person responsible for all of the deaths."

Kellen nodded, and I helped her lace her dress then opened the door to rush downstairs, passing Maeve's already empty room.

When we entered the kitchen, we found Maeve by the fire watching three eggs boil.

"Good morning, my dears. Did you sleep well?"

"Yes, thank you. Where is Sabine?"

"She left before first light."

The news stunned me.

"Hugh is going to look for help while he's in town," Maeve continued. "I hope he'll return by lunch. Until then, the best I can do for breakfast is a boiled egg. I'm afraid my fondness of kitchen labors shows in my skill."

Maeve scooped an egg from the water with a wooden spoon. She only started to straighten when the egg rolled off and landed on the floor. The shell shattered and a scramble of semi-cooked egg whites and yolk spattered her skirt.

For a long moment, she looked down and did nothing. I knew that stance. It spoke of frustration and anger. The same emotions that often plagued me when circumstances were not favoring me. Much like now. Why had Sabine left so early? It was on the tip of my tongue to ask when Kellen nudged me.

"Eloise and I can make breakfast," she said.

"Thank you, Kellen." Maeve's words were barely a whisper.

She went to the table and began brushing off egg bits as Kellen and I set to work making something else for breakfast.

"I apologize," Maeve said suddenly. "I'm making a mess of things."

"One broken egg isn't a mess," Kellen said, pouring boiling water over oats.

I measured out the honey and nuts then covered the mixture.

"While that soaks, I think I'm going to go visit Mother," I said. "I'll eat when I return."

"Don't stray from the path," Maeve said.

Her lack of argument surprised me until I recalled I had never had the chance to tell her where I'd found Anne's cap. Too smart to bring it up and ruin my chance for freedom, I gave my word, grabbed my cloak, and fled the house.

Despite the deaths, the idea of walking the woods alone didn't frighten me. While some might say it was a lack of sense, I preferred to think of it as an extra bit of sense. The forest never frightened me because it didn't feel malevolent. People were wicked, not places—the Dark Forest excluded.

My feet carried me on a familiar path to Mother's grave. The sight of the pear tree, now twice my height and in full bloom, shocked me. A small bird sang in its branches. When I entered the clearing, the bird quieted but didn't fly away.

"Hello, little friend," I said. "Thank you for singing to Mother. She loved all your songs."

I sat on the bench and sighed, trying not to let the pain of missing my mother consume me.

"It feels as if a lifetime has passed since you left us, Mother. How has it only been weeks? So much has changed. You already know that Father is gone. We thought his absence would be extensive but temporary. However, Maeve showed me something that leads me to believe he never intended to return to us. He loved you so much, Mother. But, I wish he would have loved Kellen and me enough to have stayed. We could have used his guidance."

I took another deep breath and looked around the trees. It was quiet. Peacefully so. The scent of the pear blossoms washed over me, soothing me.

"Judith and Anne are gone. Taken by magic, like you. Kellen and Maeve don't want me to pursue whoever might be doing this for fear of the Crown's angry gaze landing on us. Yet, how can I sit idly by and watch those I love be taken from me one by one?" My throat tightened as I thought of Kellen. The only person I had left.

"I'm so angry, Mother. I'm trying to control it. I'm trying to think things through and not make any rash mistakes. However, I fear this idleness is, in itself, a rash mistake. I can only hope that Sabine has reached the guard and that they will take her seriously and not imprison her."

I sighed again, looking up at the bird who was watching me from a tree limb.

"Will you sing for us?" I asked.

To my surprise, it started warbling a pretty song. I closed my eyes, letting the sound wash away some of my pain and loneliness. When the song abruptly stopped, I opened my eyes and saw Kaven approaching in the distance.

He lifted his hands in surrender and peace. Warily, I watched him enter the clearing and halt on the other side of Mother's grave.

"You look so much like her, but you are nothing alike," he said.

"Who?"

"The princess," he said.

"Prince Graydon's princess-wife?" I frowned, confused by Kaven and his current intention.

"The very same," he said.

"You've seen her?"

"A man would need to be blind not to see such beauty."

My face began to warm at such a comparison.

"For her, it wasn't just on the outside."

My mouth dropped open.

"Are you saying I'm ugly on the inside?" I demanded.

"You have hit me in the face, bashed me with a rock, kicked me in the testicles, twice, and called me a pig. I can't exactly call any of that exemplary displays of inner beauty, now can I?"

The urge to hit him again had me fisting my hands in my lap. His gaze flicked to them, and he smirked knowingly.

"Truly, I cannot decide if your intent is to kill me or annoy me. Go away."

"Why would you think I would want to kill you?" he asked, his humor starting to fade.

"Considering you knocked me from my mount, how can I say otherwise?"

He grinned anew, a show of straight white teeth, which created a dimple in his right cheek. I blinked stupidly, once more noting how devastatingly handsome he was. Kaven was dangerous in too many ways.

"Go away," I repeated.

"I fear I cannot. I came to speak with you. When we first met, you mentioned your mother's passing. That day I came to pay my respects."

I snorted.

"You came to verify I spoke the truth."

He gave me a censoring look before continuing.

"Back then, this tree wasn't even to my knee. A single stem with no branches or leaves. Yet, look at it now."

His gaze pinned me.

"This tree has been touched by magic," he said lowly. "We must cut it down before it's noticed by others."

I stared at him. At the concern in his gaze, not for me but for the possibility that magic lingered nearby and that someone else might discover it. Could his worry be real?

"That tree was the last thing my father gave me before he left and likely the final memory I'll have of him. Keep that in mind when you do what you must." I stood to leave.

"Eloise, wait. I don't mean to take memories from you. I'm trying to keep you safe."

I made a scornful noise.

"Has there yet to be a meeting between us where I did not, at some point, land on the ground?" He opened his mouth, and I quickly cut him off. "Don't bother with excuses."

He considered me for a moment then inclined his head, and I felt satisfaction that I'd won that round.

"Before your mother died, did anyone new approach you? Were you given anything?"

My first thought went to the sound of hounds in the woods and news of the Crown's impending presence. Kaven had been the first new person here. After he'd arrived, so had the messenger boy and the necklace.

"Why do you ask?"

"I'm trying to determine how a single tree, in a forest full of them, is affected so."

"Perhaps my father bought it that way," I said. "Yes, it's touched by magic. How else can it be growing like it is? Yet, nothing malevolent has come from it. You heard the bird song. This place is still peaceful despite the magic. Have you ever considered that not all magic is bad?"

He held my gaze.

"Have you ever considered that not all magic is good?"

I thought of Mother, Judith, and Anne. Anger consumed me again. Without consideration of consequence, I crossed the clearing, standing toe to toe with Kaven.

"This is our land, by order of the king, to do with as we please. If you feel we've broken some sacred law, report us. Otherwise, leave this place and me in peace before I do something I most certainly will not regret."

He made a maddened sound.

"This meeting would have been much more enjoyable if you'd been on your back again."

My mouth fell open. Before I could respond, he pivoted on his heel and stalked away. I did the same, making sure to kick every fallen branch I crossed on the way to the house.

"Vexing, officious pig," I mumbled just before I reached the door.

I took a calming breath before I stepped inside. I needn't have worried, though. The kitchen was empty save for a covered bowl of hot oats for me. I ate slowly, repeating the conversation in my head. As much as Kaven provoked me, I struggled to continue my belief he was behind the attacks. I'd been isolated in the clearing. He could have taken me like the others. Why hadn't he?

"I HONESTLY DON'T MIND the work," Kellen said, checking the tea service.

Maeve was once again with a visitor, and with Sabine gone, Kellen was determined to fix a tray.

"Besides, Sabine isn't likely to return with Hugh. I'm certain she'll want to stay until Anne is buried."

"And to ensure the guard responds," I said.

Kellen nodded, and I watched her arrange some of the pastries that Sabine had made the day before.

"Did you finish your books already?" I asked.

She gave me a wry smile.

"Are you hinting that I should be cosseted away somewhere with my silly stories instead of helping?"

"Absolutely."

She rolled her eyes at me.

"Reading, while enjoyable, isn't enough to prevent this restlessness I feel."

She caught my surprised look.

"You're not the only one plagued by that condition."

"Would you like to go for a walk with me? I should take the pig out soon."

She shuddered.

"No, thank you." I knew the shudder wasn't for the pig but for what the pig had found the last time I'd taken him out, one of the many things we'd discussed the night before.

The sound of a wagon outside had us hurrying to deliver the tea tray to the dining room for Maeve. I planned to pepper Hugh with questions about Sabine's talk with the guard. However, it wasn't only Hugh who walked through the kitchen door a moment after we returned.

The first of a pair of questionably dressed women looked close to our age. Her brown gaze swept the room and locked on us. She smiled and performed a messy curtsey. The older women, behind her, bowed her head to us while also taking in the room.

I barely noticed Hugh enter because I couldn't stop looking at the generous display of bosom that the dresses of both women offered. The younger woman's flesh trembled with her excitement.

Kellen elbowed me. Hard.

I jerked my gaze up to find both women staring at us.

"Er...hello," I said.

"These are the new maids," Hugh said gruffly. With that, he turned and left.

The sound of the door closing seemed all the louder because of the subsequent silence.

Kellen nudged me again. Someday my sister would need to find her voice.

"I'm Eloise, and this is my sister, Kellen."

"I'm pleased to meet you," the younger woman said, smiling widely again. She didn't, however, offer her name.

"And you are?" I asked.

"Oh! I'm Catherine, and this is Heather. We're very grateful for this opportunity. We're hard workers and can listen well to direction."

Her earnestness and dress made me feel sorry for her. I'd been to town enough to know the sort of employment she'd had before this.

"Then this should work out well. We eat simple meals, but due to the passing of our mother are entertaining guests that expect more refined repast. Kellen and I can show you how to make a few of the pastries, if you'd like."

"We would like that very much," Catherine said.

Kellen and I gave them a tour of the kitchen. Each time I stepped close to either of the new women, my stomach gave a lurch at the strong smells of smoke and stale booze that clung to them.

"Maeve, our guardian, will be with our guest for a while yet. Would you like to freshen up before we begin? You'll have the kitchen to yourselves, and we have a few spare dresses you can change into, if you'd like." Certainly, Judith and Anne would approve.

"We tuck away the tub just here," Kellen said, pointing

to a large cupboard to the left of the stove. "It's copper and heats nicely by the fire."

"Kellen and I can help you bring in water."

Heather gave a startled laugh.

"You want us to bathe in your tub?"

"Only if you want to," I said hesitantly.

The pair exchanged a glance, like Kellen and I often did, then nodded eagerly. However, they wouldn't hear of allowing us to haul the water. Once we showed them where the well was, they shooed us inside with a promise to have a stew ready for the midday meal within an hour.

Kellen and I snuck to our room.

"You know they're from a whorehouse," Kellen said.

"Yes."

"Don't you find that an odd occupational change?"

"Not at all. Which would you rather do? Lie on your back to service multiple men or cook for a respectable family."

Kellen glanced at her book and flushed.

"Sister, what are you reading that has you blushing?"

"A romantic book where the hero has manners and is devotedly loving to his bride. The loving is a bit detailed. She doesn't seem to mind being on her back rather than cooking."

At my wide-eyed look, she glanced at my book.

"Surely the same type of book Mr. Bentwell has been giving you."

I shook my head.

"Mine are fantastical tales of humorous adventure with happy endings for the heroine."

"Oh."

"Yes. Oh. Give me your book."

For the next hour, we read each other's books.

"This is so boring," Kellen said, closing my book.

"And this is far more than a bit detailed," I said, not taking my eyes from the page. "'He lovingly stroked her breast, toying with the rosy peak that begged for his hot, hungry mouth.' I repeat my earlier question," I said, closing her book. "What have you been reading? I can only imagine Mother's reaction to such a book."

Kellen's expression fell, and I knew I'd gone too far.

"She would have demanded to borrow it, and Anne would have scolded us for giving her something that would make her pulse race."

Kellen smiled slightly and stood.

"I'm not some delicate flower you need to protect constantly, Eloise. Although Mother was open about the joy she found in the marriage bed, I think you're right. She would probably question the wisdom of me reading about it. Likely she would think it would rob me of the joy to be found in the actual experience. However, I have no intention of ever participating in any of it. So none of that matters, does it?"

I shook my head, understanding Kellen probably better than she understood herself. She'd been hurt too much, too quickly, with the loss of those she loved. Instead of being angry at whoever took those lives from us, she pulled inward. She would rather never love again than risk the kind of pain she's endured.

Following her from the room, we quietly made our way back to the kitchen. A discreet knock on the door was answered with a cheery, "Enter."

The tub was drying before the fire, and Catherine and Heather were by the block, busily scooping a healthy serving of vegetable stew into two bowls.

"We'll bring this out to you in just a moment, miss and miss."

"We'd prefer to eat in the kitchen while there's company," I said. "And please call me Eloise. We don't stand on formality."

Catherine seemed pleased by the news, but I could see the doubt in Heather's expression. It only took a bit more coaxing for them to serve themselves and join us at the table.

"I swear to you, this is exactly what we did with our prior help," I said.

"Then, I can't understand why anyone would want to leave this position," Catherine said. "Good fortune for us they did, though."

Kellen and I exchanged a glance but didn't correct Catherine. Only time would tell if it was good fortune for them or not.

"When guests are here, Kellen and I usually take refuge

here in the kitchen as well. We mostly read these days, and we promise to stay out of your way."

"As if you would ever be in our way," Heather said.

"What do you read?" Catherine asked.

Kellen immediately blushed and kicked me under the table. I grinned.

"Books about sex," I said, mischievously.

Catherine snorted. "I doubt those books are anything like the real act. Everything's probably all pretty words and long looks. That's not the real thing. A hard cock jammed up your twat before you even have time to think a happy thought is more like it. Every now and again, a real gentleman comes along and has the courtesy to wet the way with a bit of spittle."

Kellen and I wore twin expressions of shock.

Behind us, the door opened.

"Fetch Hugh," Maeve said, her face flushed and furious.

CHAPTER SIXTEEN

CATHERINE POPPED UP FROM HER SPOT, PERFORMED HER messy curtsey, and rushed out the door.

"Send Hugh to the sitting room," she said. "Girls, go to your room."

She left without another word.

"Bollocks. I knew this was too good to be true," Heather said.

"What do you mean?"

"That there was gentry. Gentry doesn't tolerate the likes of us. Not unless it's one of the men wanting a quick fuck away from his wife's knowing gaze."

"I don't think it's that," Kellen said. "I think Maeve is upset about the topic of conversation she overheard."

"Exactly. We'll be in our own beds again before the sun sets."

The complete devastation on her face had me shaking my head.

"Not if you don't want to be," I said. "I'll go speak to Maeve. Your stew is delicious. You can cook, and I believe you're capable of cleaning and answering the door, too."

"We can do all of that," Heather said.

"Then there's no reason for you to leave."

Just as I left the kitchen, the main entry door opened, and Hugh's heavy steps echoed as he crossed the floor. He reached the sitting room before I could stop him. Unsure what to do, I hesitated in the hall.

"How could you?" Maeve's distressed tones easily reached my ears despite the partially closed door. "I cannot believe that is what you brought back. This household has a reputation to maintain."

"Forgive me, Maeve. Those were the only women I could find quickly. Maids with more experience are already employed."

"Then I hardly think you spent your time searching very wisely. I'm hard-pressed to believe there weren't two candidates more suitable for our needs in all of Towdown. You will search again tomorrow to find—

I knocked on the door.

"Come in," Maeve said, her tone still upset.

I opened the door, my gaze darting between Hugh and Maeve. Hugh looked dejected and as equally flushed as Maeve.

"I apologize for interrupting," I said. "I know the

conversation in the kitchen just now seemed questionable—"

"Seemed questionable? No, Eloise. It was entirely inappropriate for someone of your age and position."

"I understand. But, they didn't know. They do now, and I'm sure it won't happen again. Kellen and I really like them. Catherine seems very eager to please, and Heather is determined to do what she must to make this work. Please give them another chance. Their stew is good, and with Sabine still in town, we're likely to be without help for a long while, especially once word gets out about what happened to Anne and Judith."

Maeve took a long calming breath.

"Leave us, Hugh."

He bobbed his head and left the room, shutting the door tightly behind us.

"You have a kind heart, Eloise. But, please try to see things from where I stand. How would our house ever endure if guests found out they were being served by whores?"

"Former whores," I corrected. "They want to be here. They don't want to go back to what they were doing. And I question why we should care what guests think of us. Kellen and I haven't met men who inspire any thoughts of a marital bond. What then does this estate's reputation even matter? And any guest who might see Catherine and Heather and recognize them wouldn't dare speak of how they knew them, would they? Please, Maeve. Everyone deserves a chance."

She sighed, her expression of irritation fading.

"You would think that's the case, but life often disagrees."

"Come speak with them. They're a little rough, but it's nothing a bit of guidance won't smooth."

"I'm not promising they will stay," Maeve said, following me from the room.

When I entered the kitchen, Kellen was at the table with her book and Catherine and Heather were washing the dishes. The sound of the door brought all motion to a halt.

Catherine and Heather turned to face us. I smiled encouragingly, but Heather's expression said she didn't expect anything more than an order to change and leave.

"To say that I'm displeased with your presence here is an understatement," Maeve said. "The conversation you were having with two unmarried girls of good breeding is reproachable."

I cringed a little on their behalves.

"We beg your pardon, Lady Grimmoire. It won't happen again. Kellen explained that we're not ever to speak of our experiences."

Maeve glanced at Kellen, who'd shut her book and watched the exchange.

"And do you think like your sister? Do you want to give

these women a chance here, knowing what that might entail?"

Kellen looked at the table for a moment.

"I believe they would prefer to take their chances here than to return to where they were."

"She's got that right, ma'am. Please give us a chance. We'll do anything to stay. We don't mind emptying chamber pots or the like. The linens will always be fresh and your food served promptly." Catherine looked at Heather.

"You won't find more devoted help than us," Heather said, hope and desperation abloom in her gaze.

Maeve shook her head slightly.

"Don't get too comfortable. You're not suited to stay long in this house. I will put your word to the test in the days to come."

She turned toward me.

"Thank you, Maeve."

Her expression softened as she looked at me.

"Don't thank me yet. They may cause you nothing but grief in the future. It's your responsibility to teach them what they need to know. I expect no mistakes or coarse conversation after today. Now, my head aches fiercely. I must lie down."

She gave the women one last glance.

"Don't count on me for dinner."

With that, she left the room.

Catherine sagged with relief. "She's letting us stay."

"She is," Kellen said, standing. "I think we'd best show you how to make those pastries and explain any other duties you may have."

The four of us worked in the kitchen as the light outside slowly faded. Even while passing on the techniques that Judith had taught us, I listened for the sound of a carriage or horse to signal the King's Guard's arrival. However, all remained quiet outside.

When we finished with the pastries, Catherine sent us to the table to read while she and Heather fixed our dinner. I could see that Catherine was motivated and ambitious, not that Heather wasn't. She was just more subdued about it. Cautious.

Soon delectable, savory scents pulled me from my book and had me looking around the room in interest.

"Just a few more minutes," Catherine said.

The meat pies she set before us made my mouth water. The crust was golden and flakey.

"Let it cool or you'll scald your mouth," she said sitting beside me.

A moment of silence consumed the room.

"How did you become a whore?" Kellen asked.

Heather choked on her water, and Catherine patted her back.

"I don't think we should talk about that."

"Maeve's objection to the conversation was in the vivid detail," I said. "If you explain without referencing body parts, I think it will be fine."

236

Catherine looked doubtful, but I could see she didn't want to say no either.

"It just happened. There was a boy I liked. He talked me into doing things and gave me a coin after we finished. My family didn't have a lot of money, and my sister had married a goat farmer who lived more poorly than we did. I figured what I'd done hadn't been bad, and the coin was good."

Regret filled her gaze.

"It got worse, though, didn't it?" Kellen asked softly.

"It did."

"There are bad people in this world," Heather said. "People who like to hurt others for the sake of hurting them. You don't always have a choice in who you invite in."

My heart hurt for them.

"How old are you?" Kellen asked.

"I'll be eighteen this summer," Catherine said.

"I'll be twenty-three," Heather said.

I turned to my meat pie to hide my shock. Catherine looked closer to twenty-three and Heather near Judith's age. Their lives had aged them beyond their years.

Breaking open the crust, I inhaled the steam.

"This smells delightful, Catherine."

"Wait until you taste it," Heather said.

IN MY STOCKINGS, I paced the narrow confines of our room, pausing occasionally to glance out the window.

"If you don't stop, I'm going to smother you with your pillow," Kellen said without looking away from her book.

I quietly flopped on my bed.

"I'm going mad with the waiting."

"So I've noticed. The guard will appear when they appear."

"If they appear," I said, saying what we were both thinking.

Kellen sighed.

"If they didn't believe Maeve the first time, why did you suppose they would place more credence on the word of a housemaid?"

"Not her word. She had visible proof with her."

"If they even allowed her to show it. You were at that table with me while Catherine shared her story. The world isn't the kind and gentle place we would like it to be. Our parents kept us safe from the worst of it. But they aren't here now, and we need to come to terms with the reality of our lives."

I sat up and stared at my sister.

"Which is what exactly?"

She pulled her gaze from the pages to meet mine.

"The reality is that people will continue to leave our lives whether we want them to or not. Some partings will be agreeable and full of smiles. Some will be a blunt rending of our lives and filled with grief and tears like Mother's departure."

"And Judith and Anne's."

Kellen nodded and went back to her pages.

"I can accept the former but not the latter."

"Your lack of acceptance will only make the hurting worse."

Her comment and lack of emotion concerned me. Kellen was retreating too far into herself, and I worried what would happen if life continued to steal those we cared for. As kind as she'd been to Catherine and Heather, I'd noted how she'd also maintained a distance. I was the only one who remained close to Kellen. Not even Maeve had won her way in. And that troubled me greatly.

Moving to kneel beside Kellen, I plucked the book from her hands.

"And if I'm torn from your life, Kellen, what will you do?"

She shut her eyes.

"Blow out the candle, Eloise. I'm tired."

I poked her eyelid.

"No, you're not. You're avoiding the topic. Look at me, and speak your heart."

She looked at me, pain already in her gaze.

"If I lose you, there is nothing for me in this life."

It was just as I'd thought. She'd already given up and was only waiting for the end. I hugged her tightly, feeling her arms wrap around me just as fiercely.

"Our situation is not dire," I whispered. "You mustn't think so."

"Believe as you will, and I will do the same," she said.

"That's not good enough. I love you, sister. More than anyone. And because of that, we must make a promise."

Pulling back, I spoke my heart.

"If we're torn apart, the one who remains will find a way to live. Not a hollow existence but one filled with purpose and meaning that the other sister would approve of. Because we won't only be living for ourselves, we'll be living for both of us."

Tears pooled in Kellen's eyes, and I felt mine answer.

"Do you swear to do this?" I asked.

She remained silent for a very long time. It wasn't because she was overcome with emotions but rather she was considering the consequences of making such a promise. Because, I knew once she made it, she wouldn't break it. Just as she knew I wouldn't break mine.

"I swear," she said finally.

Releasing her, I smiled.

"Now continue reading your sex books."

She flushed fiercely.

"It's a wonder that Maeve allows you to read them when she so objected to the conversation in the kitchen," I added.

Kellen frowned at me.

"You're right. You don't think Maeve is bigoted toward

Heather and Catherine because of their prior occupation, do you?"

"Given her strict adherence to appearance, perhaps she is."

I stood and blew out the candle.

"I was going to read more," Kellen said, objecting to the dark.

"You haven't been sleeping enough, and it's robbing you of your good sense. The book will be there tomorrow."

Kellen grumped, but I heard her crawl under her covers.

Too restless to sleep, I undressed then went to look out the window. The stars were bright in the night sky, and I thought of Father. Was he now staring up at the same stars but from Turre? Though Kellen and I both believe his survival would be an unlikely outcome to his adventure through the Dark Forest, especially now that we knew his intent, I could only hope for his continued existence even more.

Mother would want him to live. To find happiness again. It's what she'd want for all of us.

Glancing at Kellen's peaceful outline in the dark, I wondered how either of us would find happiness. The promise I'd pulled from her had been born of desperation. A way to ensure that, if something did happen to me, she wouldn't give up on living. Yet, I couldn't help but wonder what our futures would hold if the killer was found in time for us to emerge unharmed. We would be far from unscathed.

As I stared out into the darkness, something moved in the yard below. I looked down as a cloaked figure moved across the yard toward the shed.

"Kellen," I said softly.

There was no answer. Worried one of the new maids needed something, I left my room, keeping an eye on Maeve's closed door. It wouldn't do to alert her that something might be amiss.

I slipped through the kitchen and went out the back door, lightly running across the yard in my bare feet. A flicker of candlelight flashed between the boards, and I wanted to curse. Hugh, a light sleeper, was going to notice the light, and whichever one of the pair prowled the shed was going to get caught.

The light dimmed just before I reached the outer entrance.

From inside, I heard Hugh.

"You shouldn't have come."

I bit my lip, not sure what to do. Hugh might not mention the late-night prowling to Maeve. However, if I intervened, he would certainly mention my involvement to Maeve, given his increased protectiveness.

The sound of a slap rang through the air, and my eyes widened.

"I deserved that," Hugh said.

A moment later, he groaned. It wasn't a pained groan.

Rather, the sound of it made my cheeks flush. The cold wrapped around my toes, quickly chilling me as I stood there in stunned silence.

Certainly, I had to be misunderstanding the situation.

Unsure, I slipped inside and moved closer to the boards separating Hugh's living quarters from the shed. The candle had been extinguished, leaving only the barely discernible glow from his stove.

Shadows moved within. Heavy breathing, escalating in pace, matched the rhythm of the movements. The sound of flesh against flesh made it quite clear what I was hearing. As did Hugh's words.

"You are pleasure made flesh. Let me taste you. Touch you."

The fire flared briefly. In that glimpse, I saw a woman sitting on top of Hugh. The way she moved, and the bare expanse of flesh from shoulder to hip brought to mind Catherine's words.

Frowning, I turned away from the view. A feeling of disquiet stole through me. It felt wrong what they were doing, and I couldn't place why. Perhaps it was the idea that she might think she needed to have sex with Hugh in order to stay here. I shook my head. Surely not. Maeve had been clear it was based on her opinion of them, not Hugh's.

I snuck back into the house and quickly wiped my feet on the rug before going upstairs.

"Kellen," I said as soon as the door was closed. She didn't answer so I poked her.

"I was sleeping. You told me to sleep."

"I know. But I just saw Hugh having sex with one of the maids."

She lifted her head.

"And?"

"What happens if Maeve finds out?"

"You heard Sabine. Affairs of the staff aren't important to the heads of household so long as they don't interfere with the work. I'm sure Maeve won't care."

I'd forgotten about that story from Sabine.

"What about Judith? How could Hugh recover from his grief so quickly as to love another?"

"Sex doesn't mean love," Kellen said. "And you shouldn't judge his actions. We all heal differently. Maybe what he's doing is to help him forget Judith."

I sat on my bed and stared into the dark, feeling Kellen's words hitting a tender spot in me. Is that what I'd been doing? Was I focusing on finding a murderer so I could avoid the pain quietly eating away at my insides? So I could forget Mother?

CHAPTER SEVENTEEN

I COULDN'T LOOK AT HUGH. SINCE I DIDN'T KNOW WHICH OF the maids had been with him last night, it was a little easier to speak to them. But only just. Thankfully, Maeve wasn't at the breakfast table to notice any oddity in my behavior. However, Kellen's awareness of the situation more than made up for Maeve's absence. Every time Kellen caught me studying any of the three, my shin suffered the toe on her slipper.

"Heather and I were wondering if there's a household schedule. What days are washing days? What days are supply days? And so forth."

"We go to town when we need supplies. The distance isn't far," I said.

"The linens are washed once every two weeks. When they're washed is entirely up to you," Kellen said. "The prior maid washed them only a few days ago."

"General tidying and meals are the only daily tasks," I said.

"We thought you might say that," Catherine said, sharing a glance with Heather.

"What is it?" I asked.

Heather got up and went to a cooling rack behind the block where a linen covered plate waited.

"Anyone can make a simple meal and clean a room. We knew in order to stay we would need to do something more," Catherine said. My stomach churned; and I quickly glanced at Kellen, which earned me another kick.

"We made these last night after you both retired for the evening," Heather said, carrying the plate to the table. "Would you try them and tell us what you think?"

With relief, I looked at the small multi-colored pastries daintily arranged on the plate that Heather set on the table. They were much like the lemon curd pastries that we'd shown them how to make, but with an additional dark red jam.

Taking one from the plate, I took a tentative bite. The familiar sweetness of the briarberry jam played off the tartness of the lemon curd.

"These are delicious," I said, watching Kellen take her first bite.

Hugh continued to work his way through his hot oats, purposefully ignoring us. I wondered if he'd already sampled a tart.

"Well done," Kellen said after a swallow.

"We're glad you like them," Catherine said. "We wanted to make something that might impress Lady Grimmoire. There's only these twelve, but if Heather or I could go to the market for more briarberries, we could make them for the guests."

Kellen and I looked at Hugh.

"You'll need to check with Maeve," he said without looking up.

I smiled at Catherine as Heather returned the plate.

"I'm sure she'll be fine with it." I finished my pastry and continued with the oats. Even the oats they'd made were good. I only wished Maeve had joined us so she could know that for herself.

As if my thoughts summoned her, she walked through the dining room door.

"Hugh," she said, stopping short at the sight of him. "Why are you eating in here?"

An uncomfortable silence fell as he flushed and glanced down at his bowl.

"Never mind that," she said. "I want you to go to town. The herbs I requested should be there."

He nodded and stood to leave while Maeve glanced at Kellen and me.

"Good morning, my dears."

"Good morning," we answered.

"Your timing is perfect, Maeve," I said, reaching for a pastry. "I want you to try this."

She took the small treat hesitantly.

"Why?"

"To see if it's fit to serve our guests. Kellen and I both tried it and found it enjoyable."

Maeve took a bite and looked at Catherine and Heather.

"You made this?"

They nodded.

"You've impressed me."

I grinned at Heather and Catherine.

"Since Hugh is going to town, perhaps one of them could accompany him and search the market for more briarberries."

Maeve's gaze met mine, and I was sure we were thinking the same thing. Why send one of them to town to pay coin for something we could pick from our own land?

Her expression softened.

"I think that's a lovely idea. Why don't you and Catherine go? She might need your help negotiating on behalf of this house."

I knew what she was really saying. Make sure Catherine didn't do anything to embarrass us and reveal her former occupation.

"Remember to stay together, though," Maeve added.

I glanced at Catherine, who nodded enthusiastically.

"You had better go catch Hugh before he leaves," Maeve said before leaving the room again.

As Catherine and I hurried to get our cloaks, I promised to find Kellen another book if there was time.

During the ride to town, I watched Catherine and Hugh closely. Since there were only the three of us, we all sat on the bench. Catherine had insisted I take the middle because it was more secure. However, I questioned the validity of that reason.

"I'm a bit nervous," Catherine said softly.

"Why?"

"What if someone recognizes me at the market? I don't want to bring shame to anyone."

"You won't. And you look completely different in that dress and with your hair pulled back."

"Tell me if anyone recognizes you," Hugh said. "I'll take care of it."

Catherine blushed and nodded.

The evidence of who'd been with Hugh was right there, and I struggled with how I felt about it. In the end, I decided I was glad. Kellen held everything in and was slowly dying inside because of it. I didn't want that for Hugh. If being with Catherine gave him a moment's reprieve from the pain of losing Judith, then who was I to judge him harshly. As Kellen pointed out, everyone grieved and healed differently. And perhaps their dalliance would turn into something more.

Catherine's worry over being recognized proved unnecessary once we entered Towdown. No one gave us more than a curious look. And, as we walked the market, the vendors were too busy trying to sell their goods to care who handed over the coin. Likewise, those looking to purchase goods were too occupied negotiating a lower price to notice.

A stall selling hair ribbons caught my eye. Kellen and I had ribbons aplenty to match our dresses. However, both Catherine and Heather had used bits of twine to tie back their hair.

"I think I see briarberries ahead," Catherine said.

I looked at the stall in question and cringed at the crowd around it.

"I think I'm going to wait here by the ribbons."

"Are you sure? Hugh said we should stay together."

Hugh had left us the moment he parked the wagon to fetch the herbs from the herbalist that Maeve had previously visited.

"Hugh meant in sight of each other, not side by side. We will be fine. This is the market, after all."

"I'll try to hurry." She rushed off to the group, a determined expression on her face. I knew that her urgency would not have any influence on the speed of the sale and turned to study the ribbons.

I found two pale blue ribbons that would match the color of Heather and Catherine's dresses and gave a coin to the merchant for them.

Turning, I almost collided with a familiar figure.

"You," she said. "I wasn't expecting it to be you."

"Hello again, Rose," I said, looking at the old woman. "Who were you expecting?"

She smiled, showing a row of straight white teeth that

contrasted with her weathered skin, and reached out to pat my hand. A tingle zipped along my flesh.

"Someone a bit older. What do you have there?" she asked, looking at my closed hands.

I turned my palm up.

"Ribbons for our maids. They didn't have any, and I thought they might like them."

"Aren't you a sweet child? Thinking of others. Kindness is virtuous, but it can bring trouble, too." She looked around the market. "Are you with someone?"

"My maid is just there," I said, gesturing toward the crush of people further down the way.

"Help me to that bench," Rose said. "We will watch and wait for her."

I looked at the occupied bench, ready to question her, when she hooked her hand through my arm, leaving me no other option but to help her. Not that she needed my assistance. Her steps were strong and sturdy.

When we reached the bench, she released me to glare at the two young men sitting on it.

"Remove yourselves and find something more useful to do with your time than chasing pretty skirts."

"Be gone, old woman," one man said irreverently.

The other looked at me and patted his lap.

"You can sit here, love."

Rose leaned toward the pair.

"If you act beastly, I will treat you beastly. Go!"

She said the last so loudly that the men jumped and slid off their seats, hurrying away.

Rose chuckled as she sat.

"They are so full of themselves." She looked at me. "A man can only hold what power we give them. If you never give them power, they will never have a hold over you."

She patted the seat beside her. Not wanting to appear rude, I sat. My gaze flicked to Catherine before returning to Rose, who was studying me with an uncomfortable intensity.

"Are you thirsty?" I asked. "I could fetch you something to drink."

The corner of her mouth lifted slightly as if I'd amused her.

"Would you see me killed by the King's guard?" the old woman asked suddenly. "Forced into the Dark Forest?"

"What?" I asked in surprise. "Certainly not."

She smiled again and grabbed my hand.

"Then tell me, Eloise Cartwright, why are you layered with magic?" She petted the back of my hand. "It coats your skin, clinging to you like water after a bath. What magic have you done or been near?"

I stared at her in shock. To speak so openly about magic begged for persecution of its use. Which explained her prior question. But how could she possibly know that I had been exposed to magic?

"I think magic killed my mother," I said absently, my mind racing.

If Rose could sense magic, did that then mean she could also use it? Kaven's words echoed in my mind. *Before your mother died, did anyone new approach you? Were you given anything?*

Rose's arrival wasn't before Mother's death but soon after. And she'd given me the pig.

My eyes widened as I stared at her.

"You?"

"Me? You think I killed your mother?" Rose cackled and slapped her knee. "Why would I do so? Random wickedness? No, I've had more reason to take a life and have never done so. The pig is proof. Now, why do you think I would want to kill your mother, child?"

I sighed and checked on Catherine's progress. She still wasn't any further into the crowd.

"Timing? Circumstance? I'm no longer certain. Very little makes sense to me of late."

Rose patted my hand.

"You will find that often in life. How is the pig? Did he find you anything useful?"

"Yes," I said, barely suppressing my shudder. "Though, I believe he tires of country life and would prefer to be with you."

She snorted.

"I doubt that very much."

I considered her for a moment.

"How do you know what's clinging to me?" I asked, too afraid to use the word magic.

"I think you already know the answer to that." Her gaze idly swept the crowd. "Like calls to like.

"When I sensed it in the clearing, I thought it was you using it. I wanted to see who would use magic in a place that isn't kind to those who do."

"What would you have done if it had been me?"

She considered me for a moment. For all appearances, she looked like an old woman passing time by watching the people around her, not an old woman discussing magic in the open.

"Nothing. There's no malevolence in you. However, there is malevolence here. I sense it from time to time, never long enough to find it, though. Except you. I'm curious who you would allow to use magic around you."

"Allow?" I asked.

Rose shrugged.

"Like a man, a caster can only use what power we allow them."

What she was saying didn't fully make sense to me. However, two things were clear. Rose knew about magic, and I had more questions regarding magic than I could count. Could I trust her to answer them honestly, though?

"How much do you know about magic?" I asked.

"Enough to know the magic clinging to you is too fresh to be from your mother's death. That magic still lingers at her grave."

I nodded and thought of the tree.

"Is there danger in visiting her?"

Rose glanced at me, her gaze filled with compassion.

"No, child. Speak to your mother as often as you like. There is nothing there to hurt you. Magic is neither good nor bad. Only the intent of the person wielding it."

"Can I ask you about something?"

"Haven't you already begun to?"

Taking my cue from her, I looked out over the crowd, watching the people hurry about their lives, not noticing those who might be observing them.

"Can objects kill a person?" I asked.

When Rose didn't answer, I glanced at her and found her studying me.

"What sort of object?"

"A necklace with a large stone."

"Perhaps. Do you still have it?"

I shook my head.

"It went missing."

Rose scowled at the ground for a moment.

"I met a woman from Towdown once. She told me of amulets made by a caster that protected the royal family against magic. Not long ago, I also heard of an amulet that killed."

"You did? What did it look like?"

"I do not know. I only know who the necklace killed."

"Who?"

"Prince Greydon's newly acquired wife barely a week after they'd wed."

"How long ago was that?"

"A few months."

Stunned, I looked out over the crowd and tried to find the connection. Who would want to kill a princess and my mother?

"I will be watching you, Eloise Cartwright. You have my word on that."

Rose stood with a quick pat to my knee and walked away. I stared after her, wondering if I should follow. It would do no good, though. My mind was still too overwhelmed with what I'd learned to form more questions.

"Who are you looking at?" Catherine asked, startling me.

"The old woman who shared the bench with me," I said. "Were you successful?"

Catherine held up a small bundle.

"I got the briarberries. I had to pay more than I would have liked, but I still think it's a fair deal. Is there anything else you wish to look at while we're here?"

"I think I've had enough of the market for one day. Let's go find Hugh," I said, standing.

"Do you know which herbalist he went to?" she asked.

I thought back, trying to remember the name of the shop.

"I don't think he ever said. I'm sure waiting for the briarberries took longer than the herbs, though. He's probably already by the wagon."

We'd only covered half the distance to the wagon when

I heard my name called. I looked over my shoulder and saw Hugh. He looked annoyed.

"Where are you going?"

"Back to the wagon," Catherine said. "We found the briarberries Heather and I needed. Did you find what Lady Grimmoire required?"

"Did you speak to anyone?" he demanded, this time looking directly at me.

I frowned at him.

"What an odd thing to ask. Of course I did. What's gotten into you?"

A glint of green light flashed in his eyes just before he answered.

"Nothing. You ran off last time, and I don't want to be held responsible for any mistakes you make this time."

I stared at him in shock and growing fear. A plague had found its way into my home, and I had no idea how to stop it.

Hugh turned on his heel and would have stalked off had I not caught his arm and quickly stepped in front of him. He scowled down at me, his eyes clear of any unusual light.

"Are you all right, Hugh? Did something happen to you? Did you speak to someone?"

"We don't have time for your games. Come. Kellen and Maeve are waiting."

He shook off my hold and started toward the wagon. Catherine stepped up beside me as I stared after him.

"Did you see that?" I asked.

"He was a bit abrupt. Perhaps you should mention it to Lady Grimmoire."

"No, not that. That flash in his eyes."

"Men are prone to irritabilities. Tends to happen when their needs aren't being met. A quick dip of his wick, and he'll be right again."

Confused, I looked at her.

"Sorry, miss. Didn't mean to bring up that topic. Perhaps we should catch up, though."

She hadn't seen what I had. It only made me fear what was happening all the more.

CHAPTER EIGHTEEN

KELLEN LOOKED UP FROM HER BOOK WHEN I SWEPT INTO THE sitting room and closed the door. In silence, she watched me pace.

"Sister, why are you clutching blue hair ribbons?"

The random question halted my steps.

"What?"

"In your hand. Why are you holding ribbons like you want to rip them apart?"

I looked down at the forgotten items and tossed them onto a side table.

"Never mind the ribbons. I'm going mad. Nothing is making any sense, and I need your logic."

She closed her book.

"What is it?" she asked.

I sat in a chair across from her.

"Remember the old woman I told you about?"

"The one who gave you the pig?"

"Yes. She was in the market today. She grabbed my hand and started asking me questions. She said I had been touched by magic. But she didn't think it was from Mother's death. It was more recent. I was thinking it might be from Judith and Anne's deaths, but then I saw Hugh's eyes." I leaned toward Kellen. "They flashed green like the boy's. But Catherine didn't see it. How could she not see it?"

"Slow down, Eloise. Tell me everything you saw, said, and heard from the beginning. And keep your voice down. Maeve is resting with another headache."

Kellen listened intently for several minutes. When I finished, she looked out the window.

"Having logic is only useful when the situation is logical," she said. "What purpose would the Prince have to marry a woman and kill her with a magical necklace within weeks? And for her death to be kept quiet? It doesn't make sense. We must be missing something vital. Something we're not seeing. What could possibly connect Mother, Judith, and Anne to the prince's wife?"

"Judith and Anne? They didn't die like Mother."

"Didn't they? Perhaps not from the necklace, but certainly all three died by magic. They all came from different stations in life, with the exception of Judith and Anne. And the princess, while also dying because of the necklace, met her untimely end far from here."

"Kaven," I said slowly. At some point I'd started

doubting his guilt enough that I'd stopped looking for it. Yet, there it was.

Kellen pinned me with a stare.

"You still believe it's the king's servant who is at the retreat?"

"He's the common thread. He admitted to seeing the princess, and he's here now."

"But why? What motive would he have to kill any of them? We could suppose the princess's death was an act against the Crown. Maybe because of resentment for having to serve his betters. But, that wouldn't make sense for Judith or Anne. Nor would the idea that he was a spurned lover. Mother was too old for him even if she had left the house in the last several years."

I sighed and leaned back in the chair.

"I'm frustrated to the point I want to throw caution to the wind and march over there to demand answers."

"Perhaps we could start a little closer to home and question Hugh."

I shook my head.

"He wasn't very receptive to any questions I asked during our ride home."

Kellen stood.

"Catherine was there. Perhaps what he had to say couldn't be said in front of her."

Anger beat at me at the amount of speculation surrounding the deaths and now Hugh.

"I will agree to this on one condition," I said.

"What's that?"

"If we learn nothing useful from Hugh, we go to the retreat yet today. I'm done waiting."

"I agree."

I grabbed the ribbons and followed Kellen to the kitchen.

Catherine stood by the oven, her face flushed from the heat, as she kept watch on whatever was inside.

"Are the pair of you hungry?" Heather asked. "The biscuits will be out of the oven in just a moment."

"No, thank you," Kellen said. "We're going to walk the pig around the yard."

"These are for you and Catherine," I said, setting the ribbons on the block by Heather. "I noticed you didn't have any."

"Thank you, miss."

With a smile, I grabbed my cloak and followed my sister out the door. We went straight to the shed.

"Hugh?" I called.

He didn't answer. Remembering what I'd seen through the boards the last time I'd peeked, I kept my gaze properly focused on the panel when I knocked on his door.

"Just look inside," Kellen said when we heard nothing.

I pulled the door open and quickly snuck a look inside his quarters before closing the door again.

"He's not there."

"Perhaps he's cleaning the pig's pen," Kellen said, uncertainty lacing her words.

However, he wasn't there either or raking the chicken yard or doing any of the other numerous tasks he would typically be doing this time of day. I stood in the middle of the drive and looked around.

A tingle shivered its way down my back, and I struggled not to let my temper take control.

"Not again," I said. "I won't. I refuse."

"He wasn't at the grave," Kellen said, joining me.

"We have to tell Maeve. We need to get the guards to look for him."

"Eloise, there's no sign Hugh was taken."

"He doesn't wear a cap or an apron to lose. What are you expecting to see? His pants on the ground?"

Kellen gave me a dry look.

"Well, that would certainly indicate something amiss, wouldn't it?"

"Kellen, I have an itch between my shoulder blades and something akin to a rock sitting in my stomach. I tell you, something is very wrong."

"Maeve went upstairs because she wasn't feeling well. I don't think we should disturb her because you have a bad feeling."

I saw it then. The fear in Kellen's eyes she was so desperately trying to hide. All my frustration left me. To acknowledge the fear trying to overtake her meant she would need to acknowledge the danger.

"You feel it too, don't you?"

She closed her eyes.

"Bad doesn't begin to capture what I feel. Like a knife in my breast, this growing feeling of foreboding is attempting to claim what I am." She opened her eyes and met my gaze. "Evil comes, sister. And I fear that we can no longer hide from it."

"What do you want to do, then?"

"Run," she said softly.

I pulled my sister to me and hugged her hard.

"Then that is what we'll do. Saddle the horse." Releasing her, I stepped back to pull the tack from the walls.

"Are we abandoning the rest?" Kellen asked.

I handed her the items and shook my head.

"I will collect a change of clothes for both of us and tell Maeve we're leaving. They can do as they choose."

She nodded and went to one of the stalls while I strode across the yard. It took all my control not to run. Whatever was taking the help had to be near. If it was near, it was watching. How else would all three disappear without the rest of us seeing something.

Fearful, I looked back at the shed. Was it wise to leave Kellen alone? Given that we'd just searched for Hugh separately and had both returned unharmed, I thought it was. Yet, I wouldn't chance Kellen's safety longer than necessary.

I entered the house quietly through the front door, not wanting to panic Heather and Catherine until I had a chance to speak with Maeve. Lifting my skirts, I rushed up the stairs.

I knocked lightly on Maeve's door. When there was no answer, I let myself in to wake her.

A familiar barrage of sounds, muffled grunts and groans along with slap of skin against skin, reached my ears. My steps slowed but did not stop. Drawn by the spectacle of my own foolishness, I approached the nursery door and soundlessly nudged it open an inch.

Maeve sat upon Hugh as she'd done the night before, her hands braced on his chest. Her breasts swung with each unseat and reseat of her hips over his. Hugh grunted and thrust upward to meet her, his face an expression of pleasure.

"Tell me who you serve," Maeve said.

"You. Always, you, Maeve."

"Tell me who you need."

"You. Don't leave me. I will do anything to keep you."

"Then, give me what I want."

The speed of her endeavors increased with her words. Hugh grabbed Maeve's hips and jerked into her. She grinned, a triumphant look, and her movements became frenzied. Hugh stiffened and threw his head back with a groan.

A thin stream of green light emerged from his mouth and merged with the glowing green amulet swinging between Maeve's breasts. Hugh's cheeks began to shrink in, giving him a familiar gaunt appearance.

Mother.

Judith.

Anne.

The answer to my question had been before me the whole time.

Maeve killed them all.

Silently, I backed away from the door and fled the room. How could I have been so blind? How could I have been such a fool?

At the bottom of the steps, I veered for the kitchen unable to leave Heather and Catherine to the same fate as Anne and Judith. Bursting into the kitchen, I startled the new help.

"Get out now," I whispered harshly.

Catherine's surprise turned to worry.

"What did we do, miss? Please. We'll do better."

"There's no time. You did nothing wrong. You need to leave now before she—"

The door opened behind me, and I whirled to face the threat.

Maeve walked in, pulling the sash of her dressing robe snug about her trim waist. My heart hammered in my chest, and I took a step back. The amulet hung exposed on her chest. It didn't glow now, but neither was it a dull, lifeless rock. That she wore what had killed my mother ignited something inside of me. Anger, laced with a deep pain, flayed me within.

Hugh entered behind her, bare except for the pants

clinging to his hips. His eyes flashed green when he looked at me.

I retreated further.

"Are you trying to dismiss our help, Eloise?" Maeve asked. "While I agree their backgrounds are questionable, their work has been satisfactory."

"Thank you, Lady Grimmoire," Catherine said from behind me.

"Catherine and Heather, you both need to leave now," I said calmly.

Maeve made a sound of impatience.

"Eloise, your dramatics are beneath you. Yes, you found me having intercourse with the help. It's nothing to run from. Catherine, dear, can you fix some of the tea that Hugh brought in earlier? I think we all need to have a cup while we talk."

"You can't hide behind your lies anymore, Maeve. I saw the amulet and what it did to Hugh. You killed Judith and Anne. You killed my mother. I will see you punished."

I turned and ran for the door but didn't make it more than a few steps before I was pulled back by my hair.

"Your ignorance was your protection," Maeve said a moment before Hugh hit me.

Pain exploded in my face. My knees buckled, and I fell to the floor. Maeve's next words penetrated the buzzing in my ears.

"Hugh, go outside and fetch our lovely Kellen, would you?"

"No," I whimpered, my mind clouded. Mother's last message to me rang through my mind. I needed to protect Kellen.

The door opened, and I filled my lungs to scream one word.

"Run!"

Something collided with the back of my head, and I fell into darkness.

CHAPTER NINETEEN

Pain pulled me from the depths of darkness. It radiated throughout my body, throbbing in time with my heart, only to return to my head threefold. I moved my hand to grip the offending fixture, but something rattled loudly. I winced at the sound and the unexpected weight straining my arm.

"Lie still, Eloise," Kellen said softly.

With effort, I opened my eyes and met my sister's worried gaze. Her usually pale skin was even more so. As she set a cool cloth on my brow, the momentary respite from the ache in my skull enabled me to note the fear that flickered in her gaze.

"What happened?" I asked, wincing at a new burst of pain. Why did speaking hurt my cheek? Why was I lying on the kitchen floor?

"What do you remember?" Kellen asked.

Snippets flashed in my mind. The messenger boy who delivered a cursed necklace. Mother dying and Father leaving. Judith and Anne going missing and finding the bodies, shriveled by magic. My suspicion of Kaven and the Crown. Seeing Hugh with Maeve while she wore the necklace. The same necklace that killed Mother.

A different kind of pain bloomed inside of me. A regret so deep that it bled. My mother's killer had crept into our house under the guise of comfort and support. How could I have been so blind?

"I remember enough," I said.

Closing myself off from the memories, I looked at my wrist and the metal encircling it. My gaze followed the links of heavy chain from the cuff to the source imbedded in the stone of the hearth.

"I don't recall how I became chained, though. Or why my head aches so dreadfully."

My sister turned the cloth over, replacing it on my forehead, and the coolness relieved some of the ache once again.

"I heard you yell for me to run," she said. "The horse was ready. I made it into the saddle before Hugh reached me." She swallowed hard and looked away.

I followed her gaze and saw Heather and Catherine sitting at the table, listening. Catherine's gaze met mine, and I saw her pity for me.

"For your safety, I cannot leave," Kellen said, reclaiming

my attention. "Your current suffering serves as a warning to never disobey again."

Catherine stood.

"I will tell Maeve that Eloise is awake, now." She glanced at me. "I'm sorry, miss."

Heather stood, too.

"Come, Kellen. Remove the cloth and help me start the meal."

Kellen leaned down and pressed her lips to my forehead.

"I'm sorry, sister," she whispered before standing.

My mind was too fogged with my aches for me to understand why Kellen was sorry. Especially when I was the one who'd failed us.

While Kellen followed Heather, I gingerly tried moving. My thighs ached but my knees and ankles worked without pain. My hip hurt, and I hoped it was only from laying on the stone hearth. However, when I attempted to push myself upright, the agony in my side intensified. Since sitting up wasn't an option, I rolled to my back. The contact with the stone made me hiss, and I returned to my original position.

The door swung open, and Maeve strode in. She wore the same kind expression she always had as her gaze flicked to Kellen before landing on me.

"How are you feeling, dear?" Maeve asked.

"Like I was beaten," I said, unable to keep the resentment from my tone.

"Oh, you poor thing." Concern and pity fill her gaze, sincere in every aspect of her expression and her tone.

For a moment, I was confused. She'd killed my mother and had me beaten. I couldn't breathe properly without it hurting. Was she truly apologetic?

My silent question was answered with the slow curve of her lips. The malevolent smile set my anger smoldering.

"I tried to warn you," she said. "Your inquisitive nature brought you to this. A beaten heap of human flesh before a fire." She walked toward me and squatted down, her skirts brushing my wrist.

"You could have lived a life of comfort had you only continued as you were," she said softly, her words only for me. "What you now know complicates things for you."

She lightly brushed away a strand of hair from my face, a gesture any observer might see as comforting. I now knew not to listen to my eyes.

"You're bruised and look as awful as you feel, I imagine."

She stood and primly clasped her hands in front of her.

"Life is all about appearance, Eloise. I'm afraid I cannot allow you to leave the kitchen until you once more look the part."

Maeve glanced at Heather.

"Has she said anything?"

"She asked why she was beaten and why her head hurts, My Lady."

"Nothing else?" Maeve pressed.

"No, ma'am."

"Please leave us."

Heather scurried from the room. At the block, Kellen continued to chop something.

"Look at me, Eloise," Maeve said, her voice commanding. As soon as I met her gaze, the necklace glowed, and an uncomfortable warmth wrapped around me.

"The price of your knowledge is your silence. You will not be able to speak of what has happened here. Not a single incriminating word will leave your lips. You will protect me with every remark. You may know who killed your mother, but you will never utter the words to anyone. In this, my will is your will."

The glow stopped, and Maeve turned to Kellen.

"Do what you will for her. But remember, her continued recovery lies in your obedience."

With that, Maeve left the kitchen. Kellen set the knife aside and hurried to me.

"What was that?" I asked.

"We can no longer speak of what we know."

"That she—" My throat tightened painfully, and I winced.

I tried several more times to speak about magic, Mother's death, or anything that might implicate Maeve. However, as soon as I thought what to say, my throat closed before I could speak it.

Kellen nodded as I began to understand. Maeve had cursed us both.

I wanted to rage against what had happened, but I was too weak and sore to do anything but lay by the hearth and hate. Kellen knew me well and left my side only to return a short while later with cold water fresh from the well.

"You should run," I said after taking a long drink.

She shook her head. "She vowed—"

Kellen winced and rubbed her throat, and I could well imagine what Maeve vowed if Kellen couldn't speak it. I wouldn't leave my sister either if our roles were switched.

"We must do something," I said quietly.

"You must rest," Kellen said just as the door opened once more.

Heather and Catherine shuffled in, giving us both sympathetic looks.

"Can they speak of it?" I asked Kellen, remembering I'd accused Maeve in front of them.

Kellen shook her head.

"They are silenced like us."

Catherine looked up from whatever she'd been about to do at the block.

"Not like you," she said.

"You are correct. Not like us."

I sighed and rubbed my forehead.

"Does it ache?" Kellen asked.

"Dreadfully."

"I can make you some tea."

"No. I think it best I remain aware for a while." Kellen nodded and stood.

I watched in silence as she helped Heather and Catherine prepare a meal. Despite my efforts not to think of the past, memories slipped in. How we'd welcomed Maeve into our home. How we'd given her Mother's room. My fists clenched. How we'd listened to her advice and allowed her to meet with callers on our behalves. The way I'd confided my suspicions about the Crown.

Ignorant. Naïve. Stupid.

There wasn't an appropriate name for my level of self-loathing at that moment.

As I watched Kellen move around the kitchen, I wondered about our fates. Maeve had killed Mother, Judith, and Anne, not enslaved them. Why was Maeve keeping us? Why not kill us as she had the others? But more importantly, why was she doing any of this? There were far too many questions for my aching head and far too few answers to ease any of my anguish.

Catherine disappeared into the dining room with a tray while Kellen ladled out four more portions. I closed my eyes as Heather sat at the table with her portion.

"Are you well enough to sit up?" Kellen asked from nearby.

"What purpose does Maeve have for four maids?" I asked, meeting Kellen's gaze.

I saw the answer in her eyes. Maeve had no purpose

other than that which she'd already revealed with the deaths of those before us.

Kellen's cool fingers stroked my cheek.

"I think we're different," Kellen said softly. "We have a part to play."

"If only we could see it."

"Perhaps it's better we do not."

I fisted my hands, wishing to hurt the woman who had injured me so grievously time and again.

Touching my throat, I raged against the curse that would prevent me from speaking her crimes and the chain binding me to the hearth. Unable to leave...unable to speak...Maeve likely thought I posed no threat to her. She didn't know me.

Exhaling slowly, I let the cinder of my hate grow. I, Eloise Cartwright, would find a way to stop the woman who killed my mother. And, the fire of my rage would destroy whatever Maeve sought to build with her lies and magic.

Thank you for reading Defiant, the first book in the Tales of Cinder. Eloise's story continues with Disdain. Keep reading for a sneak peak.

AUTHOR'S NOTE

Thank you for reading Defiant! I hope I kept you guessing till almost the end about who killed Eloise's mother. Have you figured out what's up with the pig yet? (Hint: Read the *Beastly Tales*! I love that I was able to write some character crossover.)

There were so many characters to introduce in this book that I created a character list for reference. This list will grow with each book so you can keep track of them all.

Eloise's suffering is just getting started. If you liked book 1, you're going to love book 2. It's so much darker, and I'll give you characters that you're going to love to hate.

If you enjoyed Defiant, please consider leaving a review. It will mean the world to me and helps the story gain visibility on the retailer sites. Without visibility, other readers will never discover this book. Without readers, there's not really a reason to keep writing. So, leave a review, tell your friends or local librarian about it, mow the title into your front lawn…whatever works.

If you want to keep up to date on what I'm working on, sign up for my newsletter at mjhaag.melissahaag.com/subscribe or join my facebook fan group, MJ's Curvy Cartel. Hope to see you there!

Happy reading!

Melissa

CHARACTER LIST

Eloise - *Cinderella* (Twin daughter of Margaret and Atwell).

Kellen - *Snow White* (Twin daughter of Margaret and Atwell).

Margaret Cartwright - Eloise and Kellen's mother.

Atwell Cartwright - Eloise and Kellen's father.

Hugh - A stablehand.

Judith - A housemaid.

Anne - A housemaid

Lady Maeve Grimmoire - Kellen and Eloise's new guardian.

Elspeth - A caster who Margaret knew.

Rose - A caster/enchanter.

Catherine - A housemaid.

Heather - A housemaid.

Aftan - The King of Drisdall

Sevil - The deceased Queen of Drisdall.

Greydon - Prince of Drisdall.

Defiant is the first Tale of Cinder, which takes part in the Beastly Tales world. If you haven't yet read the Beastly Tales, you're missing out on

a seductively dark Beauty and the Beast retelling. There's character cross over between the two trilogies that you're going to love.

Beastly Tales

Depravity

Deceit

Devastation

Tales of Cinder

Disowned (Prequel)

Defiant

Disdain

Damnation

Resurrection Chronicles

(zombies and hottie demons!)

Demon Ember

Demon Flames

Demon Ash

Demon Escape

Demon Deception

Demon Night

More to come!

Connect with the author

Website: MJHaag.melissahaag.com/

Newsletter: MJHaag.melissahaag.com/subscribe

EXCERPT FROM DISDAIN

Coming soon!

"Tell me everything," Maeve said softly. "What did you say?"

I coughed a laugh, too hurt to care that such a move might provoke her or that it sent another wave of pain through me.

"I said nothing. I wrote in the soot." It hurt to form those simple words with my bruised lips. "Told her to run. You control me through her." I shifted my gaze to look at Maeve, a slow smile curving my lips despite the pain. "Wise to chain me."

Rage filled Maeve's eyes. Her face flushed and her hands fisted as she stared at me.

"Shall I hurt her more, Maeve?" Hugh asked.

Unconsciousness would be a blessing. Instead, she exhaled slowly and regained control.

"No. Our Eloise has nothing more to tell us. Go to town and find the best tracker you can. Bring him here quickly. Do not disappoint me, Hugh."

Hugh nodded and left.

"Look after Eloise," Maeve says. "If any ill fate claims her because of her punishment, the same will befall you."

As soon as she swept out the room, Catherine and Heather both moved with speed. Heather ran outside, and Catherine grabbed the tub. I closed my eyes and drifted for a bit until strong arms gripped me.

"This will hurt, miss," Catherine said.

Suddenly I was lowered into a frigid bath. I groaned weakly and tried to lift myself out.

"Not yet, miss," Heather said. "Take a breath and go under. Let the water ease your pain."

I blinked at her, wondering if she was encouraging me to drown myself.

"Big breath," Catherine said.

I only had a moment to breathe shallowly before she pushed me under. The cold water soothed my throbbing face. Submerged, I realized most of my aches were benefiting from the treatment.

Hands tugged at me, and I emerged from the water gasping.

"Another big breath," Catherine said a moment before she eased me back under.

My vision swirled as I looked up from the water. Flames danced with shadows and faces above me. It was quiet and peaceful where I was, and I tiredly wished I could stay. The cold welcomed me, and the small inhale I'd taken escaped on a sigh.

They pulled me up quickly, and I feebly inhaled. Closing my eyes, I waited for whatever would come next, no longer caring.

"She can't rest on the stone," one of the pair said.

"I'll fetch my mattress," the other said.

Arms pulled me from the tub and back onto the floor. Each move sent more waves of pain through me, but I began to feel disconnected from it. Darkness bled through my vision, closing around me in a comforting embrace of nothingness. I welcomed it.